Bent But Not Broken

Tara Mitchell

Copyright © 2014 by Tara Mitchell. First Edition, 2014 Published in the United States of America

ISBN: 978-0-692-38270-7

This book is dedicated to my parents, Everette and Laura Mitchell and my wonderful children, Tiara, Talia, and Tavon. Thanks to all of my friends and family that have supported me during my journey of becoming an author.

I would like to acknowledge and thank my dear friend and fellow author, Robin M. Manley, for contributing her expertise and time with my first book. Thank you for all you've done.

Bent But Not Broken

Chapter 1

Like most teenage girls, Anna often day-dreamed about getting married and having children. When she was 17 years old, she met 28 year old Derrick. She thought her dreams were about to come true. Derrick was a musician at a local church. He was a handsome and hardworking man, but unknown to Anna, he was also quite the ladies' man.

Anna was hopeful about a relationship with Derrick, but she had a little problem. Anna's father was very strict. He didn't allow Anna to date and absolutely forbid any boys to come to his house, but Anna and Derrick managed to secretly talk on the phone every day. Eventually, Derrick grew tired of simply talking on the phone like some young school boy. He wanted more. He wanted to spend time with Anna. He wanted to get to know her.

"Look Anna, I love talking to you, but honey I can't stand being away from you any longer. You are my woman and I want to see you," Derrick said.

Anna felt chills running all over her body. No man had ever called her a "woman." She had never even been called "girlfriend." She felt wanted and she suddenly felt like a woman. She wanted to spend time with Derrick-her man.

"What do you suggest? You know my dad will never let you come over here. He won't even let boys my age come to the house. If he knew I was talking to a man 11 years older than me, he would kill both of us," Anna said as she glanced out the window to see if her father had left for work.

"Why don't I pick you up after school? I don't have to work tomorrow night," Derrick said.

"I have to be home when my dad gets here, but...but, maybe I could leave school early," she hesitantly suggested.

"Skip school, hummm. Well, we could spend the entire day together. But why wait until tomorrow? I don't go to work until 7 p.m. tonight. I can pick you up and have you back in time for you to get home before your warden; I mean your dad gets home."

"Well, I guess you could pick me up at the back of the school. I'm sure no one will see me getting into your car back there. I will meet you in about 30 minutes."

"Okay." Derrick happily agreed.

Anna quickly finished getting dressed. She made a quick trip to her mother's room to use some of her expensive perfume and red lipstick.

When Anna got to school, she made a point of not being noticed. She walked in the front door and out the back door. Derrick was already there waiting. Anna quickly got into his car.

"Good morning baby," Derrick said, knowing that young girls like Anna desired to hear words like baby, my woman, and sexy. "I think it would be best if we go somewhere so you won't be seen. We wouldn't want anyone who knows you to see us. They might tell your dad that you were not at school today. I wouldn't want you to get in any trouble with your pops sweetheart. What do you think?"

"Sure, where do you suggest we go?"

"Well, I would normally suggest that we go out to eat or maybe a movie, but it's too early for a movie and unless we go out of town, it's not a good idea to go out to eat either. Not to mention, if we do go out of town, we won't have much time together." Derrick paused as if he was trying to figure something out. "We could go to my apartment, but I live with my brother and we won't have any privacy. My brother's girlfriend will probably be there too."

"I don't mind. I would love to see where you live, besides I would be too nervous to be alone with you anyway Derrick."

"You are always safe with me. I would never do anything to make you feel uncomfortable. You are too special to me and I think the world of you."

Anna smiled as they drove to Derrick's apartment. When they pulled into the apartment complex, Anna felt knots in her stomach; actually a little queasy. She felt like an adult and a little girl all at the same time. Derrick parked and quickly jumped out of the car and rushed around to open the car door for Anna.

When they got inside Derrick yelled for his brother, but he didn't answered back.

"I know he told me that he was off today. We were supposed to visit my mom before I go to work," Derrick said as he walked down the hall and peeped into what appeared to be a bedroom. "Anyway, make yourself at home sweetheart," he said as he walked from down the hall and into the kitchen. "Did you eat breakfast before you left home? I can fix you something."

"Yes, I had some cereal and orange juice, but can I have a glass of water? My throat feels a little dry."

"Of course honey, and if there's anything else you need from me, just let me know," Derrick said in a soft, romantic voice.

He grabbed a bottle of water out of the refrigerator and joined Anna in the living room. He opened the bottle and gave it to her while staring in her pretty brown eyes. She was so nervous she slowly drank the water to avoid talking.

"Is everything all nice and wet now?" Derrick asked. "A dry throat can really be irritating."

"Yes."

"Yes, what?" Derrick questioned with a smile on his face.

"It's all wet. I mean I'm all wet… I mean my throat feels better." Anna was getting frustrated and tense. She could feel changes going on in her body. She wanted to leave, but she didn't want to disappoint Derrick.

Anna held onto the empty water bottle until Derrick gently took it out of her hand.

"Do you want to be with me as much as I want to be with you?"

"Yes, I guess so," Anna replied. She was not sure what Derrick meant by "be with." She wanted him in her life because she wanted a boyfriend, but she wasn't ready for anything else. At least she didn't think she was ready.

"Good, let me show you something," Derrick said as he grabbed Anna's hand and led her down the hall.

"Why are we going back here?"

"You'll see," he said as he opened his bedroom door. "We'll just lie down on the bed and watch a movie. That way I can rest up a little before I have to take you back to school. I have to work tonight remember?"

"I guess that will be okay."

Derrick put a movie in the DVD player and kicked his shoes off and motioned for Anna to do the same. They laid on the bed and cuddled as they watched TV. Derrick pulled Anna closer to him and began stroking her long hair. He made small talk and pretended that he was into the movie. He whispered in her ear and kissed her fingers. Anna could feel her body tingling all over. She wasn't sure what to do. She was confused. She wanted to leave and she wanted to stay. She wanted him to keep touching her and she wanted him to stop. She wanted to kiss him, but she was afraid that she wouldn't be able to stop. She turned her head slightly toward him to see if he was watching the movie. He was looking at her.

"Did I do something wrong?" he asked.

"No, not at..."

Before Anna could finish her sentence Derrick kissed her like a man kisses a grown woman. Anna didn't stop him. She wanted him as much as he wanted her.

Chapter 2

"I'm not going to school today," Anna told Derrick when he called to see if she wanted him to pick her up from school. It had been three months since the first time she skipped school to be with him. It had become a regular routine. Sometimes she would get up early and go to Derrick's apartment before school and only miss homeroom, sometimes she would leave during lunch time and return an hour later, and other times she would check out early.

"Why not? No, don't tell me. Let me guess. You're finally going to let me take you out of town?" Derrick questioned. "I know it's been a while since we've seen each other. This new work schedule is crazy."

"Actually..." Anna tried to think of something to tell Derrick. She didn't want him to know what was really going on with her. "I feel as if I've not been getting enough sleep lately. I've been staying up all night trying to make up some homework. I just want to sleep in today."

"Oh, I see. Okay, I will call you later. Get some sleep, my love."

"Thanks," Anna said and hung up.

My love? That's funny. Seems as if I haven't been his love for a few weeks now, Anna thought as she got dressed. Anna suspected that she was pregnant, but she didn't want to say anything to Derrick until she was sure. She went to the local health department and found out that the morning sickness and daily fatigue she was experiencing was indeed symptoms associated with pregnancy. Anna was terrified not only because she was pregnant, but also because of her father's warning. He told her that if she ever got pregnant or even got close to a man, he would literally kill her. Anna didn't know where to turn or who to turn to. She ultimately decided to call Derrick, although lately he only seemed to appease her on the phone and claimed that they were going to be together soon. When they did make plans something would always come up and plans had to be cancelled. If they did meet, it was never for long. Anna didn't really expect Derrick to answer the phone. Anna tried to decide what she would say if he answered.

"Hello," a woman's voice said. Anna assumed it was Derrick's brother's girlfriend, although she had never met her or Derrick's brother.

"Hi, can I speak to Derrick please?" Anna asked.

"Whatever you want to tell him, you can tell me!"
Anna was shocked. "Just tell him I'm pregnant," she said quickly realizing now that this woman must be Derrick's new girlfriend. She had heard that he was messing with someone else, but he denied it.

"Ok little girl. I'll tell him," she said and hung up.

Anna felt betrayed as she hung up the phone, but she was determined not to get upset. She was more concerned about her parent's reaction. Anna wasn't sure how she was going to break the news of her pregnancy to her parents. Anna was their only child and they had high hopes for her. They had already planned her future. Anna knew that this news was going to be the most disappointing thing she ever had to tell them. Anna decided she would tell her mother first.

"Anna what were you thinking? Have you totally forgotten everything we taught you about remaining a virgin until you get married?" Mrs. Lauren, Anna's mother, cried uncontrollably while listening to Anna's devastating news. Anna felt like storming out the door and running away from home, but she couldn't. As the time ticked away, she experienced many different emotions. She felt fear of what her father would do to her, anger that Derrick had a new girlfriend and sadness as she thought about her mother's tears. None of her fears compared to the fear she felt for her life. She knew that telling her father was not going to go well at all. At noon, Anna expected her father to come home for lunch as he had done for years. She knew she had to tell him whether he killed her or not, he had to know. Anna's father, Mr. Jay, came home for lunch, sat down and began to eat his Big Mac meal as he usually did.

"Don't you need to tell your daddy something?" Anna's mother asked.

The tears began to roll down Anna's face as she thought about the disappointing look she was about to receive from her father. Anna cried even harder when she thought about the many years her father had kept her under control with the threat of death.

"Daddy, I'm going to have a baby," Anna blurted out.

Mr. Jay looked at his wife to see if she displayed any inclination of this being a joke. She looked at her husband with sad, tear filled eyes and simply told him,

"It's true. She's pregnant."

Mr. Jay put his food down and dropped his head. The tears flooded his eyes, rolled down his face, dropped to the floor, and disappeared into the carpet. Anna had never seen her father cry. Mr. Jay sat in his chair uttering something about his virgin daughter and what she had done to him, to herself, and to their good family name.

"Daddy I'm sorry," Anna said as her own tears continued to flow.

As Anna walked across the stage at her high school to receive her high school diploma, she could feel her baby growing and her plans to attend college to become a pharmacist dying. It seemed like the last few months of her pregnancy flew by so fast that she didn't have time to prepare for the arrival of the newest family member, baby Danielle.

Without questioning the paternity, Derrick signed the birth certificate and diligently paid child-support. The checks were helpful, but they were not enough. Anna's dreams of getting married and having at least four children diminished to just being a good mother and providing for her daughter.

Anna's mother agreed to keep Danielle so that she could work. She began working a full-time job in the manufacturing industry. It wasn't the life Anna had dreamed of, but it seemed to be working out better than she thought it would. Mr. Jay had finally accepted the fact that he was a grandpa and was actually happy to have Danielle around. He got up most nights to prepare bottles, change, and rock Danielle back to sleep. Anna was pleased to see her father so accepting of his new granddaughter. Anna wished Derrick was the one doing those things, but other than paying child-support, Derrick had nothing to do with Anna or Danielle. He was too busy building a life with his new wife. Anna heard that he was bragging to his friends about the fact that he and his wife were expecting a baby. Anna was upset that he took her virginity and then just walked away from her as if she never meant anything to him. She thought about taking Danielle over to his new house so that he could see how beautiful his daughter was, but Anna decided that she was not going to do anything to cause any drama in his life or hers. She was content being a single parent and just wanted to start a new life of her own, in her own home. She began saving money. On her days off she would get up as if she was going to work, but actually go house/apartment hunting.

"Mama I'm moving out," Anna blurted out one day as she helped her mother dry the dishes. "I found an apartment on Sunset Avenue." Anna paused to get her mother's reaction. When her mother didn't respond right away, Anna continued. "It's not the best looking place, but at least it will be ours; Danielle and I. I'm eighteen now and besides, I feel like Danielle and I are a burden to you and daddy."

"Anna I don't really.....I just don't think you should leave. At least not right now. You're too young." Anna's mother finally said as she dropped the dish back in water. "I can tell you this baby girl; it is not easy being a single parent and living all alone with a newborn child. What about work? How are you going to work and raise Danielle on your own?"

"Ma, I have two jobs and I'll get a third one if I have to. I can do this. I just need you to help me. Can you just continue to babysit Danielle until I find daycare? That would really help me out." Anna talked non-stop as if she had it all worked out. "I'll pay you every week. Think about it, you always say that you wish you had your own money so you wouldn't always have to wait on daddy to give you some. You don't even have to tell him when I give you the money. It could be your rainy day fund. Please ma, it will really help me a lot. If things don't work out I might have to move back home, but at least let me try."

"I guess you think you're grown now. Well, if that's what you want to do, I guess I can't stop you." Anna's mother sighed as if she was reluctant to agree, but she knew that Anna's mind was made up. "Okay. I'll help all I can, but you're going to have to tell your father."

"Thank you Mama," Anna said smiling at her mother. As they finished washing dishes in complete silence, Anna knew that her mother really didn't want her to move out.

Anna worked two and sometimes three minimum wage jobs and at the same time, she was constantly looking for better opportunities. By the time she was twenty-two years old, she had finally gotten a decent job. Even with a better job, a decent car, and a comfortable life for her and Danielle, Anna still felt like something was missing. She was constantly looking for true love, but she always seemed to end up in dead end relationships and was left feeling as if her heart had been trampled on.

Anna didn't seem to have any problems getting a man's attention. The problem was she always seemed to attract the wrong men. She was an attractive, reserved young lady with sweet voice and a pleasant personality. She was voluptuous, and her curves were just where they needed to be on a woman. Men seemed to fall for her and women seemed to resent her, so there always seemed to be some type of drama going on. She really didn't want any drama, especially on her new job.

Anna had not been on her job long when she met Paul. He was a material handler. She thought he was very handsome. She didn't see much of him at work because he was always moving merchandise from one department to another. Whenever Paul got a chance to take a break he would conveniently take it while Anna was on her break. It was obvious that he was interested in her. Anna was young, but she knew that whoever was to win her over had to be a hard worker, loyal and a man who loves children. Paul appeared to be an ample candidate.

Paul began to flirt with Anna on a daily basis. He would buy her breakfast and drinks throughout the day. He always joked with her and put a smile on her face. She began to feel very comfortable around him. She was becoming very interested in Paul and it wasn't long before he asked for her phone number. Their co-workers began to suspect that Anna and Paul were becoming more than just co-workers and then the rumors began to circulate. Anna noticed that people, especially the women, were giving her strange looks when they thought she wasn't looking. She wasn't sure what was going on, but she assumed it was because they were jealous that Paul was interested in her and not them.

One evening after work Anna called her friend Kay, who worked in another department. Anna began to tell her about her new interest at work.

"Paul?" asked Kay. "You do know his wife works right in front of you?"

"His wife? Are you kidding?"

"I have been on that job for over 3 years and one thing I do know is Paul is not going to leave his wife. I heard that they are having problems, but girl trust me, that don't mean nothing," Kay said.

"I appreciate you for telling me. I guess that's why those busy body women were staring at me. They could have just told me," Anna said.

"They probably thought you knew and just didn't care that he was married. In companies like this where men and women work alongside each other all day, people tend to get real close. Some men spend more time with other women than they spend with their wives. We see it all the time; work place affairs. Half the couples you see at work have spouses at home. Paul just happens to be one of those that works at the same company that his wife works at. That is why people are staring at you," Kay explained. "You need to just forget about him. That's trouble waiting to happen."

"Well, once again thanks for being honest with me. I have to go. I'm going to give Mr. Paul a piece of my mind."

"Girl, don't do that. You don't need to give anybody a piece of your mind; you need all the mind that you have."

"Ha, ha, ha!" Anna laughed. "I'll remember that. I'll talk to you later," Anna said. She didn't wait for Kay to say goodbye before ending the call. Anna couldn't wait to confront Paul. *"He really has some explaining to do,"* She thought as she waited for him to answer the phone.

"Hey Paul. I have a question for you and please don't lie to me." Anna began without waiting for Paul to greet her. Are you married and if so, please explain to me why you didn't tell me? For heaven sakes your wife works at the same company with us. What the heck were you thinking? Wait, I guess you weren't thinking. You definitely weren't thinking about me."

"Baby, I didn't think you would understand our arrangement. We are separated. We still live in the same house, but we don't sleep together. I sleep on the sofa and she sleeps in the bed. We haven't had sex for months. It's over. I'm just waiting for her to find her own place. Really Anna, it's nothing to it. Just trust me and let me handle this. Do you honestly think I would be so stupid as to date someone I work with knowing my soon-to-be ex-wife works with us. I just don't go around telling everybody because I didn't want any other woman in my face. Those women out there are so needy and desperate." Paul paused to give Anna a chance to respond, but she didn't, so he continued. "When I saw you, I just couldn't resist you. It's was just something about you that made me risk everything."

"So what do you expect me to say? I'm supposed to just keep dating a married man knowing that I want a husband of my own, is that what I am supposed to do?"

Anna knew it wasn't a good idea to continue dating Paul. She wasn't sure if she should trust him or not, but nevertheless, she followed her heart and continued to let her relationship with Paul evolve. She knew that one day she was going to have to face Paul's wife. She knew that a hardworking man like Paul was worth keeping and she knew that Paul's wife probably thought the same thing. Anna and Paul continued to see each other at work.

One day as Anna was on her way to the cafeteria for breakfast, she was suddenly approached by a co-worker. The co-worker looked as if she had just seen a ghost. Anna really didn't know the woman's name, but she had seen her on another production line before.

"Girl I saw Carla, Paul's wife, in the bathroom. She was looking though her purse trying to find her lipstick. She pulled out an ice pick. I jokingly asked her why she had an ice pick. She said she was going to stab any woman she saw with her husband. She said it as if she was joking, but I think she was really upset. I heard her say something about sorry women sleeping with another women's husband deserve what they get. You better watch your back!"

"Let me tell you something. I might be quiet, but if a fight is what she wants, a fight is what she'll get. I guess no one ever told her not to bring an ice pick to a gun fight." Anna paused. She knew it wasn't a good idea to admit that she had a gun in her purse. "Well today a nice blade might come in handy. I don't want to have to load up on the job, but if I must, then I must."

Anna cut her break short and went to find Kay. She tried to tell herself that Carla had no reason to be upset with her. Paul was the one that betrayed her. *"I don't owe her any loyalty; I'm not married to her. He is,"* Anna thought as she walked up to Kay's work station.

"Kay, take this check in case you need to bail me out of jail because something serious is about to go down. Someone overheard Carla making threats. I take every threat seriously and I will defend myself to the end."

"Girl, she's just hurt. She knows she has really lost him now. I'm sure she ain't going to do nothing," Kay said as she took Anna's check.

"She needs to target her anger at her husband, not me. If she thinks I'm going to run from her, she have another thing coming. She better know what she's getting herself into. This ain't what she wants. Anyway Kay, let me get back to my side of town. Just pray that I don't run into her. I might not be afraid to fight, but I'm not going looking for a fight either. See you later."

The day passed by smoothly without any signs of Carla. Anna was anxious for lunch time to arrive so she could tell Paul what was going on. As the time seemed to slowly tick by, Anna began to think about what Paul must have to deal with at home. She imagined that Carla was probably fussing at him every day because he had a girlfriend while still living with her. One thought after another ran through Anna's head. She wondered if Carla would try to get Paul back. *Maybe that is why she is suddenly making threats. Maybe now she sees what a good man he is,*

Anna thought. Anna had been so engulfed in her thoughts of Paul and Carla's home life that she didn't even realize that it was time for her to go to lunch until one of her co-workers walked by.

"You coming Anna?" the co-worker questioned and kept walking.

"Save me a seat. I have to go to the little girl's room first," Anna said as she walked to the bathroom. As soon as Anna entered the bathroom, the door opened and a few co-workers walked in. They spoke, washed their hands, and they quickly left. The door opened again, but Anna didn't look up to see who entered.

"Are you sleeping with my husband?" A woman blurted out as Anna stood in the mirror combing her hair.

Anna didn't bother turning to face the women. She knew it was Carla and she knew there was no point in denying that she was sleeping with Paul. The rumors had been circulating for months. Paul had even told Anna that he and Carla had argued about the rumors several times.

"Well yes I am. It's my understanding that you and Paul are separated," Anna replied.

"Listen, that man comes home to me every night," Carla said as she took a step towards Anna. "So how long have you been sleeping with him?"

"I know where he sleeps at night; On the sofa." Anna said as she turned to face Carla.

"Yes, that's right, he told me." Anna said and then looked away from Carla long enough to search for her lip gloss. She turned to the mirror and slowly applied a fresh coat of her red blossom #2. When she finished, she addressed Carla again. "You and I both know that he is just waiting for you to find you some place to go." Anna glanced at Carla's reflection in the mirror for a few seconds and then turned to face her. "As for how long he and I have been making love to each other? Well, that's none of your business. You and Paul are separated and I don't have to explain nothing to you," Anna said as she tossed the lip gloss back in her purse.

Anna turned and walked towards the second bathroom stall. She really had to go, but she wasn't going to go while Carla was still in there. She wanted to pull out a weapon so Carla would leave, but she didn't want to take a chance on losing her job.

"You know what Carla...nevermind. Now if you will excuse me, I have to take care of some business. I really don't want to keep rattling on and on with you," Anna said hoping that Carla would just leave her alone. "So I suggest that you turn around, you and your tiny ice pick, and walk out the door before you and I both be looking for a new job. Just know I'm not standing here empty handed, if you know what I mean. I'm with Paul so get over it and by all means hurry up and find some place to go!"

Carla was so angry she tore the steel bathroom door off the hinges while storming away. "You want him, then have him. You ain't got much and in time you'll see. I'll just keep Chris. See, Paul ain't the only one that can keep secrets and a lover or two. I've had mines for two years," Carla said as she snatched the bathroom door open and left. Anna wasn't sure what Carla was rattling off about as she stormed away. Carla was breathing so hard that Anna could only hear part of what she was saying.

Anna was just glad Carla attacked the bathroom door and not her. She didn't want to have to shoot Carla, or anyone for that matter, but she would have taken her down if she had to. Anna let out a sigh of relief once Carla was out of the bathroom. When Anna walked in the break room she could tell that her co-worker had heard or saw something. *"Maybe Carla ran through here in a rampage after she stormed out the restroom,"* Anna thought. Anna grabbed her lunch out of the refrigerator and sat down. She looked at her watched. She only had a 30 minute lunch and she had just wasted 15 minutes of it in the restroom. She quickly ate her lunch and returned to her line. She was disappointed that she had not seen Paul on her break. She walked back to her line thinking about what she would say to him if she saw him. She passed the line that Carla had been working on for the past week, but she had not returned to it yet. She hated that Carla had been moved closer to her, but she had to deal with it, because she was not going to request to be moved, nor was she going to quit.

Anna had been on her line for over ten minutes when she saw Carla return to her line. She looked as if she had been crying. Anna tried not to look in Carla's direction, but she didn't want any surprises. Anna looked up in time to see Carla suddenly drop her work tools and walk off the line.

"Guess she couldn't take it no more," a co-worker said as they watched Carla head towards the front door." She's only been with Paul for eight years and has had a lover for the last two years.

"What are you talking about?" Anna asked.

"You see, she might claim to be hurt, but that woman ain't just hurt because Paul is with you. She has secrets of her own. Well she thinks they're secrets. The real twist is her lover has more secrets then she does."

"Secrets?" Anna asked with a confused look on her face.
"Have you seen today's paper?" the co-worker asked as she passed Anna the Daily Times. "Look at the wedding announcements." The co-worker pointed to a picture of a man and woman in the wedding attire. "Carla's lover just got married. Yes, Carla was in a real love triangle. That would make me walk out to. I guess that's why she didn't say much to you at first."

"You know what? While she was confronting me in the bathroom she said something about Chris and two years.

"Chris is...well, he used to work here. I remember hearing about that. But girl there is more. She has also been seeing Samuel."

"Who is Samuel?" Anna asked.

"Paul's best friend or at least they use to be best friends. I'm not sure if they still are or not. Don't even know if he knows they mess around."

"Paul suspected that Carla was cheating," Anna said. "I thought he just told me that so he wouldn't seem like such a bad man because he was cheating on her with me. He never mentioned anything about suspecting his best friend."

Shortly after the confrontation, Carla left Paul and their seven and nine year old daughters and moved in with Samuel. The girls were easy to love. Anna developed a strong bond with Paul's children and treated them as if they were her own. They really seemed to love being with Anna; however, they missed their mother and wanted to live with her permanently. Paul didn't want to let them go, but it was obvious that they were unhappy without their mother. Paul gave Carla custody of the girls, although it hurt him deeply.

Anna wasn't sure why her coworkers always gave her funny looks, especially since they knew that Carla and Paul both did each other wrong. They seemed to hate the fact that Anna was with Paul. Her work performance began to decline and she was constantly getting warned about production and tardiness. When Anna's supervisor called her into the office early one morning Anna knew she was about to get fired.

"I got you," Paul told Anna when she informed him that she had lost her job. Anna didn't want to depend on him so she filed for unemployment and put in job applications right away. She was determined that she was not going to move back home or be dependent on a man. Luckily she found another job in no time.

"Look Anna, I know things will be easier for you once I get my divorce and make you my wife," Paul said when he called Anna on her lunch break. "What do you think about that?"

"I hope that's not your way of proposing to me, because if it is you need to work on that between now and the time your divorce is final."

"What if I told you my divorce is final as of today?' Paul replied. "Anna there's just something about you that's so different from other women. Of course you're funny, you're easy to talk to, you give me all the attention I need, you cook for me, you're a great mother, you're very intelligent, a great dancer, a wonderful singer and a hard worker, but that's not it...there's something else about you that draws me to you."

Anna didn't know what it was, but she had heard it before and of course she was happy to know she had that kind of effect on men, especially Paul.

"Where have I heard that before? Do all men use the same players handbook?" Anna asked sarcastically.

"Maybe, but real players don't fall in love and this –as you call us- player is in love with you and wants you to be his wife. Paul stared in Anna's eyes. "I'm serious Anna. I love you and I want you."

Chapter 3

Shortly after Paul and Carla were divorced, Anna and Paul got married. Anna's dream of being a wife had finally come true. She was excited about fulfilling her role as a wife and step-mother to Paul's children. She was extremely happy but the honeymoon stage would not last long.

Several months into the marriage things began to get shaky. Paul started receiving a lot of late night phone calls. He suddenly didn't want to spend time with Anna on his days off. He would come up with any excuse to leave. Anna was tired of being left alone.

"I need to take your ca to get an oil change," Paul said one Friday afternoon. He grabbed Anna's keys from the key hook. "I probably need to get a back tire as well."

"Okay, but where are your keys? Don't you have a key to my car?" Anna asked, thinking that she would be stuck at home if he took his set of keys and hers. "What if I want to go somewhere?"

"I can't find my keys and I need to get there before they close. My keys are here somewhere, I just don't have time to look," Paul said and headed out of the house as if the discussion was over.

Paul had been gone for 5 minutes when Anna heard the doorbell. "Don't tell me you've lost my keys too," Anna said as she opened the door. She was shocked to see a strange woman standing there and the woman seemed just as shocked to see Anna.

"May I help you?" Anna asked the woman.

"Uh, yes..well...Hi." The woman stood there as if she suddenly didn't know what to say.

"Who are you?" Anna waited a few seconds for the woman's response, but she stood stiff as if the cat had her tongue. Anna continued to question the woman. "I've seen you passing by my house several times a week for the last two or three months. "Are you new to the neighborhood or are you looking for someone?"

"I'm sorry. You just startled me a little. Anyway I work with Paul and umm I also sell purses. Paul mentioned that you like purses and you might want to buy one or two from me."

Anna didn't take kindly to this woman just showing up unannounced, nor did she believe her purse story. "No," Anna said as the woman began to explain that she had several styles that she might be interested in. "I really don't know why Paul would tell you that. I'm not really a "knock-off purse" kind of woman. I only buy originals."

"Oh well I'm sorry, maybe I got you mixed up with someone else. I would have never bothered you if I had known that," the woman said with a smirk on her face.

"Perhaps you should consider calling your referrals next time. That way you don't waste your time or your gas showing up at people's houses for nothing." Anna just looked at the woman with a smile on her face. "Now if you will excuse me, I have to get back to my daughter."

"Oh you have a daughter? How old is she?

"Yes I do. Hence the word "originals", Anna could tell that the woman had a ulterior motive. *"Maybe she is looking for Paul,"* Anna thought. As she stood at the door talking to the woman, Anna noticed that she seemed to be looking past her shoulder.

"Where's your daughter? I would love to see her."

"She's like her mother. She doesn't like strangers so goodbye! By the way, just because you only see my husband's car in the driveway doesn't mean he's home or that I'm not here. I will let him know you stopped by."

Paul's behavior began to get strange. He was gone a lot more and often claimed that he was working overtime. Anna suspected that Paul was lying about working more hours. She called his job late one night and was told that he wasn't there. When Anna questioned Paul about it, he stated that whoever answered the phone must not have seen him. His behavior was constantly changing. He started listening to different kinds of music. He started eating different foods. He even changed the kind of underwear he wore.

Anna was about to back out of her driveway when she saw a familiar car passing by. It was the same car that belonged to the woman who that randomly stopped by with the knockoff purses. She watched the woman pass by and turn down the next street. Anna quickly peeled out of the driveway and followed the woman. The woman pulled into a driveway several miles away. *"So she drives all the way to my side of town just to come by my house,"* Anna thought. "Well if she can pop up at my house the least I can do is return the favor. Anna parked her car beside the street and walked up to the woman's front door. Her screened door was open and Anna could hear the woman talking on the phone. She was just about to ring the doorbell when she heard something that made her pause.

"Paul I told you one time I don't want to be around your wife. Just let me know when she's gone and I can come over and take a look at the washing machine. I don't want any problems and she looks and acts like the type that will start something." Anna listened quietly before she finally rang the doorbell.

"Hold on Paul. Let me see who's at the door," the woman said as she peeped out the window. "Oh my God! It's your wife! I'll call you right back."

"So…that wouldn't happen to be my Paul you were just talking to on the phone was it?"

"What are you talking about lady?"

"I heard your entire conversation. I already know it was him." Anna quickly snatched the woman's cellphone from her hand and pushed the screened door closed while she held it closed with her body. Anna just needed one minute to look through the call history. Anna hit the button for recent calls.

"So you were talking to my husband. Just like I thought."

"Look Anna May. All we were talking about was a washing machine that he said you were trying to sell. I was going to come see it but I wanted to come while he was home. Honestly that's why I stopped by a few days ago."

"Why didn't you mention that when you came by? Why tell lies about some pocketbooks? Anna was fully aware that the woman was not telling the truth.

"I didn't know if he had told you about me or not, besides, I wanted to come while he was there."

"What is it about you to tell?" Anna paused. "Lady, I don't buy this story for one minute and I really don't have time for the games." Anna heard the woman's home phone ringing. The lady quickly disappeared to answer it. Anna turned and walked away. There was nothing else to discuss.

When Anna got in her car she realized she still had the woman's cellphone in her hand. She quickly used it to call Paul.

"Hey sweetheart. Are you okay? What happened?" Paul asked.

"I happened," Anna said, knowing that Paul wasn't expecting to hear her voice.

"If the only reason this home wrecker came to our house was because she wanted to buy the washer, why does it matter if I'm there or not? And why the hell are you calling her sweetheart?"

"Anna please calm down. See that's one of the reasons why she didn't want to come over while you were there. She heard that you are very insecure and crazy and..."

"Crazy? I'm not the one that's crazy. She is and you are too if you think I believe that cockamamie story y'all telling. Why do you talk to her so much if all she wants to do is buy the washing machine? Anna pulled back in her own driveway. She put Paul on speakerphone and began roaming through the text messages. "Wow!" Anna said as she read a text from Paul.

"What?" Paul questioned Anna, noticing she wasn't saying much.

"I will talk to you when you get home." Anna hung up without saying goodbye or responding to Paul's question.

Anna read a few more text from Paul and she checked the call history. They had talked several times that day and texted back and forth since 2 a.m. that morning. Everything she read was very inappropriate being that they were only communicating about a washer.

Anna didn't want the woman to file a police report claiming she had stolen her phone. She waited until Paul came home that night and told him she had to take a drive to clear her mind. She drove back to the woman's house and placed the phone under the driver's side back tire. *"She'll think twice the next time she decides to mess around with a married man."*

Anna questioned Paul several times about the woman and their relationship and he assured Anna that he would never cheat on her. He reminded her of how bad it hurt him to find out that Carla had cheated on him and that he would never want to do that to another person. Anna wanted to believe him but it was hard to do.

Shortly after the arguments began to calm down, Anna started having some problems. She complained to Paul that the cheap soap he bought was irritating her vagina and she couldn't get any relief. Even a three-day treatment of Monistat didn't help. Paul didn't seem to be too concerned about her irritation and seemed to dismiss it all together. Ironically, Paul approached Anna the next day and said, "I made you an appointment with your gynecologist, Dr. Thomas, so you can get that problem checked out." Anna's first thought was that her new husband was being thoughtful and wanted to make sure she was okay. *"Not many men would be thoughtful enough to make their wives a gynecology appointment. Hmmm...maybe they would if they already knew what her problem was,"* Anna thought.

The nurse told Anna that her symptoms could be caused my perfumed soaps and dyes and it didn't necessarily mean her husband had given her anything like she thought. Anna felt relieved and began her seven day treatment of antibiotics.

Seven days after Anna's doctor's appointment, she received a phone call from the Dr. Thomas's office.

"Mrs. Paxton?" the nurse asked.

"Yes, this is she."

"Dr. Thomas wants to see you tomorrow at 3:00 p.m. Are you available at that time?"

"Sure. I'll be there."

Anna tried to figure out why the doctor needed to see her. She wondered about it so much that she couldn't sleep at all that night. She made sure she was at the doctor's office promptly at three o'clock. As Anna arrived at the doctor's office she saw her husband's car in the parking lot. She checked in and the nurse directed her to Dr. Thomas's office where her husband, Paul was already sitting. Dr. Thomas greeted her and asked her to have a seat beside her husband.

"Mrs. Paxton have you finished taking your antibiotics?" Dr. Thomas asked.

"Yes," she replied.

"Mr. Paxton have you finished taking your antibiotics?" he asked Paul.

"Yes sir," Paul said.

Anna was confused and looked at Paul in dismay. She couldn't figure out why Paul had been taking antibiotics because the nurse told her she could have been having the symptoms because of soaps and dyes. Paul never told Anna he was taking any medication. She didn't understand what was going on. She looked at Paul in total confusion.

"Dr. Thomas," Anna said as she stared at Paul. "What is Paul taking antibiotics for and why wasn't I told anything about it until now?"

"Well, you both have an STD and that means one of you gave it to the other," Dr. Thomas explained.

"Wait one minute," Anna said as she rolled her eyes at Paul and then turned to Dr. Thomas. "Dr. Thomas, your nurse said that the irritation that I was feeling could have been caused from that cheap perfumed soap that Mr. Romance here bought me or dyes in my under clothes."

"Typically that's true," Dr. Thomas said as he looked at Anna and then at Paul. "I am sorry, but that's not the case this time. One of you have been unfaithful."

Anna knew she had not been unfaithful to Paul. When she married Paul, she made a commitment to be faithful to him for the rest of their lives. Anna didn't want to hear anything more. She hurried out of the office, leaving Paul sitting there with a stupid look on his face.

Anna returned home and packed her belongings. She left Paul and went back home to her parents. "This will always be your home," Anna's mother told her. Anna was happy to hear that, but she instantly missed the independence of running her own home verses submitting to her parent's rules again. Anna wanted to feel like a wife again and not a little girl living with her mommy and daddy.

After a couple of weeks Anna and Paul decided to try to make their marriage work. Anna wanted him to feel that he could be honest with her and that they could work through anything. She wanted the truth about the affair, so they could start over with no secrets. However, Paul still denied that he had cheated on her. It continued to be a wedge between them. The cycle of on again off again developed and continued for years, but Anna remained faithful to Paul. She loved him and wanted to be with him more than anything.

Eight years into the marriage Anna and Paul's marital problems became even more critical. Anna was working third shift at a local pharmaceutical company. Her mother was faithful to her promise to always help with Danielle whenever she could so Anna would drop Danielle off at her mother's every night. One night after Anna dropped Danielle off, Anna's best friend Renee called her before her shift to see if she wanted to buy some DVDs. Anna didn't have the extra money so she called Paul to see if he had any. It was strange that Paul didn't answer the phone so Anna felt something was wrong. *Maybe he went to sleep early. He does have to work in the morning,* she thought. She made a quick U-turn and headed back to the house before work to see if Paul was okay. When she arrived, Paul's car was gone and all the lights were off in the house. *"What is he up to now?"* she asked herself. She decided to call in sick and wait for Paul. She was suspicious because he didn't answer his cellphone and that was very unusual. *What if I was calling him because my car broke down,* she thought? Anna thought back to Paul's demeanor before she left for work. He was fully dressed, even sitting around with his brand new Tim's on. He was wide awake which was unusual at that time of the night and he kept checking his watch.

Anna parked her car a few blocks from her house and then called Renee to pick her up. Anna waited patiently in the dark house. At 3:30 a.m. she heard Paul open the front door. He went straight to the kitchen and began rattling what sounded like a bag of food. *Fast food, no doubt,* Anna thought. He obviously had worked up an appetite. Anna came from the bedroom and met Paul in the doorway of the kitchen. He was completely surprised to see her.

"Why are you here? Why aren't you working and why are you in a dark house?

"Nevermind that Paul! Why are just coming in at 3:30 a.m. and where have you been? That's what I need to know!

"My buddy Steve called me to pick him up from across town. He had been drinking so I picked him up and took him home."

As Paul was talking Anna noticed some unusual looking spots on his neck. Upon closer investigation, Anna saw that Paul had a necklace of passion marks all around his neck.

"Woman you are seeing things! I haven't even been around a woman much less let one suck on my neck!

Anna lightly turned Paul's head to get a better view and he immediately slammed her into the wall, choking her and calling her a crazy bitch. Anna was furious and wanted to fight back, but she knew she couldn't beat a man and she didn't want to go to jail for shooting him. When she was able to regain her balance, she ran out the house. She was so mad she walked several blocks in the dark and frigid cold to her car.

Once again, Anna and Danielle ended up staying with her parents for nine months. She had had enough of Paul's cheating. She could no longer tolerate his disrespect.

Anna gave up on her marriage and this time she decided it was time to start seeing other people. She joined an online dating site and in no time at all she met a young man that captured her heart. They chatted and talked on the phone for eight months before they decided to meet in person.

Anna and Brian met for dinner and he took her shopping right away. He was not a very attractive man, but he too was a hard worker, a college graduate, and he was very respectful. He catered to Anna's needs and desires. She liked that about Brian, but it didn't really impress her like it would the average woman because she was used to being taking care of financially. Anna and Brian began to talk more frequently and even began to see each other every weekend. Anna was beginning to forget all about the fact that she was still legally married. She felt like a free woman, but it wasn't long before Paul called Anna and gave her an ultimatum.

"Anna, you've been gone for nine months and I want you to come back home. I've asked you before, but this is the last time. You either come back this week or I'm moving on." Anna really liked Brian, but she still loved her husband and she thought she owed it to the both of them to try one more time. Anna and Danielle moved back home with Paul. They were relieved to be back in their own space once again.

Brian didn't want to let Anna go and really couldn't comprehend why she would go back to a lying, cheating husband when he was doing all he could for her. Anna continued to communicate with Brian and occasionally she would sneak away to spend time with him. They had not been intimate, but the more time they spent together the more they wanted each other. She began to fantasize about being with him. He made her feel desired and sexy. She wanted to feel that way with Paul, but she couldn't get past all his cheating. Anna wanted to know what it would be like to actually be with a man that made her feel the way Brian made her feel.

One day Anna and Renee went lingerie shopping. Anna bought several bags of matching bras, panties, and cute teddies. She even bought a few cute dresses and a sexy pair of heels. She thought about Brian as she shopped. *I wonder if he would like this,* she asked herself. The mere thought of Brian was making Anna feel sexy. She imagined what it would be like being with him for the first time. *Hmmm, well look at this,* Anna thought as she looked at her phone ringing. She smiled when she saw Brian's number pop up. Anna told him she was out lingerie shopping with her friend.

"I want to be your inspector," Brian joked. "Why don't you come by for a little while and show me what you've bought?"

"Ok baby, I can work that out. My friend has an appointment later on anyway and I was going to wait in the lobby but I'll get her to drop me off at your house instead. How does that sound?"

"Great sweetheart and just tell her that you have some private business to attend to while she sees the doctor."

"You know she's my best friend. She knows all about you baby. Don't worry about a thing. I'll be there shortly."

Renee dropped Anna off at Brian's house in Raleigh. She laughed as Anna reached in the back seat and grabbed all of her bags of lingerie. "Girl, don't do nothing I wouldn't do, Renee said as Anna proudly walked up the sidewalk to Brian's door. Brian greeted Anna with a kiss and took the bags of lingerie from her sweating hands.

"So let me see what you bought baby," Brian said to get Anna's attention. He could tell that Anna was preoccupied as she entered. Anna looked back a few times as she entered the house. She didn't want Renee to be mad with her for backing out of their girl's day out and letting her go to the doctor alone.

"Come on lovely lady. Follow me. I want to see your selections."

Anna followed Brian into the bedroom. She emptied her bags on Brian's bed and he went through every piece, holding them up and examining every inch. Brian picked out a teddy that he liked.

"How about you try this on so I can see how it looks on you."

Anna hesitated, but she went to the bathroom and put the teddy on for Brian to see. Anna was a little ashamed of her large frame, but Brian seemed to love it. He grabbed her by the waist and pulled her close to him. They began to kiss passionately, something they had never done before. All sorts of thoughts began to flood Anna's mind. *"This is not right,"* she thought. *I have never had sex with anyone but Paul since I married him."* Anna wanted to remain faithful to her unfaithful husband but she couldn't turn away now. Brian removed the spaghetti straps off Anna's shoulders and began to kiss her all over her neck and breasts. He laid on his bed and Anna playfully straddled him while asking him if that's what he really wants.

"You're a grown woman Anna. I know you can feel this. You know exactly what I want and I can tell you want it too," Brian said. Anna and

Brian made hot, passionate love for the first time and it felt wonderful. Anna felt loved and desired once again.

Anna returned home that night as if nothing had happened. Paul was watching television and dosing off, as he often did on Saturday afternoons. She slipped past him with her bags and put her lingerie in the bottom of her lingerie drawer. She didn't want Paul to think she had just been lingerie shopping so she strategically placed some shoes, a dress, and a handbag on the bed for Paul to see. It was getting late so Anna began to prepare a late night snack for her and Paul to eat. Anna hoped that Paul wouldn't want to make love to her that night. *How would it feel to him? Would he be able to tell if she had sex with another man? she thought.* She started complaining of body aches and headaches. She thought Paul would sympathize with her and give her a sex break. To no avail, as soon as they got in bed, Paul wanted to make love. Anna couldn't say no.

Only a few days had passed since Anna and Brian were together and she couldn't get him out of her mind. She thought of him every second and every hour of every day. Anna felt guilty for cheating on Paul with Brian and she was more surprised that she had managed to get away with it so easily.

One Tuesday morning before going to work, Paul told Anna he was going to the doctor to see why he had been having a strange feeling in his penis. He told Anna if she had given him anything he would kill her. Anna wasn't experiencing any symptoms, but she knew that didn't mean she was in the clear. She was scared. Anna left before Paul came home from his appointment. When he returned, he called her to come home because they needed to talk.

"Talk about what Paul?" she asked.

"The doctor told me you gave me something," he said.

"I didn't give you a damn thing. How could I? I have been faithful to you Paul. I'll be home in a few minutes."

Anna called Brian to see if he had any symptoms of an STD. She hoped he would be honest. He said he was fine and he knew for a fact he didn't have anything. Anna was afraid of what Paul might do. She took her time going home. Paul called her again and demanded that they need to talk right away.

When Anna got home, Paul opened the door before she could get her key in the lock.

"Sit down," he said.

Anna hesitantly sat down, not knowing what Paul would do.

Paul suddenly moved his leather jacket that was lying on the sofa. Under his jacket was a double barrel shotgun. He stood over Anna with the shotgun in his hand, demanding that she tell him who she had been cheating on him with. Anna started crying and pleading with Paul not to kill her. He was very angry and didn't seem to hear anything she was saying.

"No one! No one Paul!" She kept yelling. He had two huge shotgun bullets in his hand. He loaded them into the gun right in front of Anna's face. She was screaming and begging for her life.

"I'm giving you one more chance to tell me who he is!" Paul shouted.

Anna began to talk none stop, trying to explain and reason with Paul.

"Ok! Ok! It was just someone I met. You and I were not together when I met him. You had given me that STD, I know it was you because I was always faithful to you, so I know I didn't get anything from anyone else. I met him while I was staying with my parents. I was mad and hurt because I loved you with all my heart and you cheated on me. I was just with him that one time. I promise you Paul that is the truth. One time, but I don't love him. I just did it to get back at you. I hate what I did. I'm so sorry Paul. Please don't kill me! Please, please don't kill me! I have Danielle to raise. She needs me!

Paul pointed the shotgun at Anna's face and pulled the trigger! The shotgun jammed up and Anna took off running for her life. She got in her car and drove straight to the police department. The officer filed a report and sent two other officers to the house to talk to Paul. The police arrested Paul and confiscated his shotgun and a 9mm handgun he had hidden in the closet.

Paul stayed in jail that weekend which gave Anna some time to try and figure out what to do next. She felt her parents were tired of her running back home, so she didn't want to impose on them again. Anna and Danielle went to stay with her aunt for a few days. Anna went to the doctor to get treated for whatever she had given Paul only to find out she didn't have anything.

When Paul got out of jail, he started calling Anna apologizing for his behavior. He wanted her to come back home once again to mend their marriage. He told her that he didn't have a disease, but he knew she had cheated and he just wanted to scare her. Anna didn't want to go back to Paul after that ordeal. It took a lot from her mentally and emotionally. She didn't have any money in her savings account to get her own place and she didn't want to keep running to family for a place to live. Reluctantly, Anna ended up going back to Paul but everything seemed different. She didn't trust him because of the cheating, but now she feared him and she didn't really want to be with him anymore.

Chapter 4

Anna's health began to deteriorate. She was diagnosed with cardiomegaly, high blood pressure, and diabetes. She suffered from menorrhagia along with other complications that women generally experience. She had gained over 150 pounds during her ten years of marriage. The weight was affecting her back, knees, and her mental state. Since her early teens, she suffered from depression and it was getting worse. Anna's marital problems, excessive weight gain, health condition, and stress on her job caused her to have a breakdown. She thought she could depend on Paul to help her feel better, but he only added to her stress. Paul told Anna she was not a woman because she couldn't have a baby for him. Anna was devastated. Paul's comment made her feel less of a woman. He was constantly insulting her and picking fights, mainly about her not being able to have his child.

Anna went on a personal journey to get pregnant. She wanted to prove to Paul that she could have a baby. They both had children from prior relationships, but they couldn't seem to have any together. Anna had heard there was a gynecologist in a nearby city that would possibly put her on Clomid, a fertility medication. She didn't hesitate to schedule an appointment. The doctor put her on Clomid for a couple of months and Anna still didn't get pregnant.

Anna discussed fertility options with her doctor. She referred Anna to a fertility specialist in Chapel Hill. Anna faithfully kept her appointments. She would leave her home at 5:00 a.m. to be at her appointments by 8. She never told Paul she was seeing a specialist. After her first three appointments and undergoing several tests, the doctor wanted to test Paul because he didn't see any obvious reason why Anna couldn't get pregnant; therefore, before they could go any further Paul had to be seen. Anna didn't want to tell Paul she was spending all her money and some of his on a fertility specialist, so she decided not to go back again. She went back to traditional methods of trying to get pregnant.

Anna suffered two miscarriages over the next few years. She became more and more depressed and it was taking a toll on her well-being. Anna was constantly crying, lying in bed all day, and eating herself into a frenzy. She would go to work and get so emotional that she would have to leave. She eventually got fired from her job because of her attendance and tardiness.

Anna felt her life was falling apart. She didn't have any hope of seeing better days. The tears continued to pour from her eyes. She began muttering to herself, *"I am such a failure. Pregnant before I was eighteen years old. Everyone else left school and headed to college. They have degrees now, good jobs, nice homes, and I got a miserable marriage, no job, and paying rent for a house I will never own. They enjoyed college life, clubbing, and frat parties. The only party I got to experience was potty training Danielle. Lord, why did I throw my life away? I just can't take*

this. Will it ever be my time to live? Will I ever enjoy my life? I'm no good

for nothing or no one! Lord, am I being punished for something? I just

can't do this...I would rather," Anna couldn't say it. She cried

uncontrollably as she stumbled to her feet.

She went into the kitchen and got a bottle of prescription pain

pills from the cupboard. "This will stop the pain," she said as she took

pill-after-pill-after-pill. "I just need to stop the pain for a little while," she

said as she continued taking the pills." She drank a glass of water to

flush the pills down. She had consumed more than half of the bottle of the

high potency pain relievers. "What is the point of living? It's hopeless,"

she said as she grabbed the bottle and began taking the rest of the pills.

"Who would want to keep living such a horrible life?"

Anna did not think about the pain she would cause her family,

especially her daughter Danielle. She did not think about her parents and

how devastated they would be if they lost their only child. Anna did not

think about an eternal life in hell. She just wanted to end the hurt and

pain she was experiencing inside. Anna just wanted to be free from the

mental, physical, and emotional abuse delivered by the man she once

loved with all her heart. Paul walked in the house just in time to see his

wife collapse and fall to the floor.

"What's wrong with you?" he angrily asked. He stepped over Anna

and headed towards the living room. He looked back to see if Anna was moving. "What a way to welcome me home after a long night at work. I could have stayed at work if I wanted drama."

Anna was conscious, but she could not speak. Paul made a phone call.

"Hey Ma," Paul said when Anna's mother answered the phone. He didn't give her time to say anything. "Something is wrong with your crazy daughter. I just got off work and came home to find her over here laying in the floor. I am tired and I don't feel like fooling with her. Can you come see what's wrong with her?" he said and hung up the phone without waiting for a response.

Ten minutes later, Anna's mother and her best friend arrived. She walked in and saw her daughter lying on the floor. Paul was just sitting there shaking his head. Anna's mother and her friend got Anna up and took her to the emergency room. Her mother showed the nurse the bottle that the pills were in. They immediately sent for a machine to pump Anna's stomach. Right before the nurse returned with the pump, Anna threw up all over the bed and floor. Anna's mother immediately began asking questions. When the room door opened everyone looked back to see if it was Paul, but it wasn't.

The hospital Social Worker walked in. She stated she just had a few questions for Anna and her mother. She asked one question after another. Anna tried to answer in a way which would cause the social worker not to think that she was suicidal but instead desperate for some relief from her pain. The social worker didn't seem to buy Anna's story completely and set up an appointment with a psychologist the following day. There were so many questions to be answered. Only Anna knew what triggered this reaction. Only she knew how low she felt and the inner hurt that had been tormenting her for so long. She felt as though she had been to hell and back. She wasn't happy with Paul, she couldn't carry a child, she lost her job, her health was failing, and her weight was spiraling out of control.

Anna's weight had reached over 300 pounds. She could no longer stand for more ten minutes and she could only walk a few steps without getting extremely winded. She was diagnosed with sleep apnea and she often struggled to breathe. She didn't anticipate living much longer, but despite the suicide attempt, she did want to live. She just wanted to live a better quality of life. She wanted to be healthy and happy.

Anna heard of a weight loss procedure called a gastric bypass. She read all the reviews. Some were favorable and some were not. There was a small percentage of deaths related to having the surgery. She initially thought that she wouldn't be able to go through with something so invasive. After careful thought and consideration, Anna discussed the operation with her physician and went for a consultation with a bariatric surgeon. After talking to the surgeon, she decided that she needed to seriously pray about it. She did not want to make such a life changing decision without discussing it with someone that could give her some good advice. She wasn't sure who to talk to about it, but she knew she needed to talk to someone.

Months later, Anna's hairstylist invited her to attend the church's Family and Friends Day, where she was the Pastor. Anna had not been to church in a long time and thought it would be a good idea to seek some spiritual guidance. There was something missing in Anna's life and maybe she could find it at church.

Regardless of all Anna's health concerns, Paul and Anna's marital problems were improving. After six years of faithfully attending church and letting the past stay in the past, their marriage seemed to be on the right track. It almost seemed too good to be true. Paul had stopped asking Anna about having children. Anna thought about the fact that she was getting older and Danielle was about to graduate high school. Anna was focusing on her associate's degree and was planning to start back in the workforce.

Anna wanted to work, but her weight was literally holding her down. She had to lose weight. She decided to go forward with the gastric bypass surgery. She figured either way, having the surgery or not, she could die. It was a tough decision, but having the support of her husband, her parents, and Pastor Elms made the decision easier.

On the day of Anna's surgery, her husband, daughter, parents and her pastor were all with her. They all sat patiently in the waiting room trying to console Anna. She cried the whole time as she waited for the nurse to call her. Anna really thought she might die during the operation. When she was called back to get prepped for surgery, the family was allowed to walk back with her. Pastor Elms led them in prayer before they rolled Anna into the operating room. It was something about Pastor Elms's praying that always seemed to comfort Anna even in her worst times.

The surgery went great, but Anna had to stay in the hospital for monitoring for three days. She was ready to get home to her own bed. Anna's mother and Danielle made sure the house was clean. They made sure that Anna had everything she needed. Anna had to adjust to a new way of eating, but she knew in order to see a dramatic change she had to go to the extreme. She exercised every day and ate healthy. In less than a year, she lost over 150 pounds. Anna's health had greatly improved. She no longer had to take all the medications she had been taking. Anna was feeling much better about her life. The only health issue that Anna's was experiencing was severe bleeding. Even though she had dealt with this issue for about 13 years, she had faith that one day that she would be healed. She constantly prayed about it.

During Sunday service, Pastor Elms invited the entire church to join in on a fast leading up to Easter Sunday. Anna truly believed that the inner peace and comfort she had experienced over the past few years was because of her faith and faithfulness to God. That Friday Anna sat at her kitchen table and began to read this passage from the King James Bible:

Mark 5:25-27

And a certain woman, which had an issue of blood twelve years,

And had suffered many things of many physicians, and had spent

all that she had, and was nothing bettered, but rather grew worse,

When she had heard of Jesus, came in the press behind, and

touched his garment.

When Anna got to that scripture she thought about all she had

been through having the same issue. *Lord if I were there I would do the*

same thing. I would just touch your garment, Anna thought to herself.

Anna immediately felt at that moment that she was healed. She got up

and went to the bathroom to discover that all the blood was gone! Anna

couldn't wait to tell what Jesus had done, little did she know that some

people would call her crazy for believing it. Anna knew that even in these

modern times that even she could receive the same healing from God.

When she returned to her kitchen table, Anna continued to read the rest

of the passage...

Mark 5:28-34

For she said, If I may touch but his clothes, I shall be whole.

And straightway the fountain of her blood was dried up; and she

felt in her body that she was healed of that plague.

And Jesus, immediately knowing in himself that virtue had gone

out of him, turned him about in the press, and said, Who touched

my clothes?

And his disciples said unto him, Thou seest the multitude

thronging thee, and sayest thou, who touched me?

And he looked round about to see her that had done this thing.

But the woman fearing and trembling, knowing what was done in her, came and fell down before him, and told him all the truth. And he said unto her, Daughter, thy faith hath made thee whole; go in peace, and be whole of thy plague.

Chapter 5

Anna's life continued to improve. She graduated from the community college with an associate's degree in Medical Office Administration and because of her outstanding academic performance, one of her professors personally lined up several job interviews at local medical facilities for her over the next two weeks. Anna was overly excited to be on the right track with her career goals.

"Paul honey, when my internship ended last week with Dr. Patel she hired me on a permanent basis as her office assistant. I really love the job but do you think it's feasible for me to drive so far everyday just to have enough money for gas and food? She's only paying a little over minimum wage. What do you think I should do? I really want to be able to contribute to the household more but I don't see that happening with this kind of pay.

"Anna, don't worry about the bills here. I can take care of everything until you find something closer to home. Who knows, maybe you'll get hired at one of your interviews. Just relax about it baby. I got you."

When Danielle graduated from high school, Anna was proud of her and pleased that she had never gotten into trouble. She always had excellent grades in school and received numerous awards for her academic success. Anna smiled every time someone told her what a fine young lady she had raised. Anna felt as if Danielle's graduation was not just an end of a chapter in her daughter's life, but a beginning to a new chapter in her own life. Anna was planning to further her education, get another job, and travel the country with or without her husband.

Anna hoped that Danielle would go off to college after graduation, but she did not. Even when Anna found out that Danielle had decided to delay college for a while, Anna was still hopeful that she could travel and enjoy herself. Danielle had not lived the ideal childhood. She had witnessed a lot of the mental and physical abuse that her mother had endured. Anna wanted Danielle to at least live a normal young adulthood. She did not want her daughter to end up like her. She did not want Danielle to give up on her dreams.

When Danielle began to complain about feeling sick, Anna feared that Danielle might have the flu. Everyone was getting sick with a cold and flu like symptoms, even Anna. She dreaded going to the doctor, she purchased some cheap over-the-counter medications. She was not surprised that they didn't seem to help. A week went by and everyone began to feel better, everyone except for Anna. After two weeks she was still miserably sick. She had no choice but to see her physician. After a week of prescription meds and antibiotics, Anna still felt horrible. Anna had not called her friends in over a week. She was appreciative that they constantly called Paul or Danielle to see how she was feeling. When her friend Michelle called, Anna was feeling a little better so she decided to talk to her. They talked about the issues they both were having in their marriages and then Michelle began to analyze Anna's illness.

"So," Michelle said. "The doctor diagnosed you with the flu and now after almost two weeks you're still not feeling too much better? Seems like something else could be wrong."

"In a nutshell," Anna replied.

"Have you taken a pregnancy test?" Michelle questioned.

"Pregnancy test!" Anna said and chuckled. "Girl we tried for years to have a child, but I finally gave up and have not thought about it in years. My baby is eighteen years old and out of school and I am ready to live it up!"

"They say that once you stop stressing over it, that's when it happens," Michelle paused and chuckled. "I think you're pregnant!"

"Yeah, right! If I'm pregnant you can be the Godmother," Anna replied.

Michelle and Anna went back and forth joking on the subject.

"Ok, looks like I'm going to have another Godchild," Michelle finally replied. Anna and Michelle talked for a few more minutes before Anna began to get sleepy from the medication that she had taken. She explained to Michelle that she needed to take a nap and said goodbye.

The next morning while Paul was at work Anna's mind kept drifting back and forth to the conversation she and Michelle had the night before. *What if I'm really pregnant? I know I'm not. I can't be. Not after all these years,* Anna thought to herself. *But what if I am? What if I am pregnant?* The thoughts kept racing through her mind. *What the heck, I'll go buy a test anyway.* Anna still was not feeling good, but she really needed to go to the pharmacy. She grabbed her keys and rushed out of the door. She bought the cheapest pregnancy test she could find and headed back home.

The directions stated that 'for best results use the first morning urine.' It was midday, but that didn't matter to Anna. She took the pregnancy test anyway and got an immediate positive result. *Ummm, this can't be right,* she thought. She went to Danielle's room and told her she needed to send her to the pharmacy.

"What do you need ma?" Danielle asked.

"I just took a pregnancy test and it was positive, I don't think it's right, but I want to make sure. I need for you to go buy another test."

"Ma! I don't want to go buy a pregnancy test, can you please go?"

"No Danielle! Go on now," Anna persisted.

Danielle grabbed her mother's car keys and walked out of the house. She was only gone fifteen minutes, but to Anna if felt like hours.

When Danielle returned with the pregnancy test, Anna didn't hesitate taking it from her hand and headed to the bathroom. She was anxious to see the results. She took the test and once again the results were positive. She still couldn't believe she could be pregnant. Anna called her gynecologists' office and was told that she could come in anytime for a pregnancy test. She didn't want to say anything to Paul until she knew for sure, so she went to the doctor's office to take another pregnancy test. The test came back negative and Anna was disappointed, but relieved to get the final say from a doctor's office.

"Mrs. Paxton, your test was negative but may I ask why you thought you were pregnant? the nurse asked.

"I've been sick for about two weeks. My doctor prescribed different medications that would normally help but this time nothing has made me feel better. I don't even remember when I had a period but I took two over-the-counter pregnancy tests today and they were both positive."

"Oh, well in that case, it might to better to do a serum pregnancy test. These tests are more reliable in detecting an early pregnancy. All I need to do is draw a little blood Mrs. Paxton."

The test came back positive. Anna was really pregnant.

Only two days after giving Paul the good news, Anna believed she was about to miscarry. Anna had miscarried before, but at that time she didn't even realize she was pregnant. This time she knew, she had proof, and she even had a due date. Paul took Anna to the ER to see if they could stop the bleeding. The doctor examined Anna and ordered an ultrasound. Anna and Paul waited anxiously to see if the baby was still alive. When the doctor finally came in the room, with a smile on his face, he told them that he had good news and bad. *If he had bad news why was he smiling?* Anna thought. *I guess we will soon find out.*

"Well, the good news is that you're still pregnant and what you're experiencing is implantation bleeding. Come with me," he said. "I want you both to look at this screen. You see those two white dots? Those are embryos. You're pregnant with twins."

"Twins," Anna and Paul said in unison.

"Yes, twins," the doctor said.

Tears immediately fell from Anna's eyes and rolled down her cheeks. Paul looked as if he had just seen a ghost. They both looked at the other in shock and total disbelief. After all these years and failed fertility treatments, Anna was pregnant with not one, but two babies.

Over the next eight months Anna and Paul's life was filled with joy, gratefulness, excitement, and anxiety. They prepared for the arrival of their precious gifts. They faithfully attended every doctor's appointment and scheduled ultrasounds. They bought two of everything, decorated the babies' room, and watched every TV show that came on about giving birth.

Anna's pregnancy was considered a 'high risk pregnancy' because she was over 35 years old and she was carrying multiples. There was a major concern that she may not be able to carry the babies full term. One of the babies was closely monitored for a few weeks because it was not growing at a normal rate. Anna was really concerned and ultimately she began to have a lot of doubt. The baby eventually started to grow and ultimately outgrew the other baby, weighing more at birth.

Anna and Paul were doting parents. They both seemed extremely happy and did not even seem to be bothered by the midnight feeding.

Paul's participation in the rearing of the children, did not last long and Anna's joy didn't either.

"Anna, what is wrong with you?" asked Paul. "Ever since you had the babies you've been crying and upset all the time. What is going on? You don't want the kids or something?"

"Of course I want my kids! Are you stupid?" Anna exclaimed. "I'm just tired! I'm up all night every night. When one baby goes to sleep the other wakes up and I'm just tired Paul. You're asleep all night because you have to work and I understand that but my God! I just need your help like you did the first few weeks. Everyone that promised to help me has abandoned me. I'm just overwhelmed!"

She couldn't even pay for a little help with the kids. Anna was reaching 40 and her patience was not the same as it was with Danielle. She was eighteen when she had Danielle. Anna began to experience post-partum depression, so her doctor placed her back on a mild antidepressant and recommended counseling. Anna didn't feel like she needed counseling. She just wanted some help with the kids and some time to go out alone, even if it was just to the grocery store.

Paul started to realize how much stress Anna was experiencing and he often told her to go somewhere when he got home from work. Anna really needed this time alone and it gave her room to breathe, but she felt guilty for wanting to be alone. *I wonder if I'm the only woman that feels like this,* she thought. *"I see women everyday with their kids and they seem so happy and content, but I don't feel happy. It's not that I don't love them because I really do, I'm just not happy,"* she thought to herself. "Lord when I wanted kids, so badly you didn't allow me to have them, but now I'm an old woman you give me two. *Why Lord?" she questioned.* "Lord tell me how to handle this."

A few days after asking for help, one of Anna's childhood friends, who had four children, stopped by.

"How do you go out with all those kids by yourself? I mean they're all under 5 and you don't seem to have a problem," Anna questioned her friend.

"Girl, if I wait on somebody to help me, I won't ever go nowhere or get anything done. I just throw them all in the car and just go!"

"I have so much I need to do, but I cannot seem to get any help," Anna explained.

"Look, from now on, put the babies in the car, grab the double stroller and do what needs to be done."

Anna took her friend's advice and decided that she was going to get out of the house. She took the babies to Wal-Mart alone for the first time. She parked beside the cart return rack, grabbed a cart, and placed both car seats in the cart with the diaper bag and went shopping. Anna couldn't believe how easy it was to actually be out with the twins and without Paul. *Whew! What a relief, she thought.*

The winter season came and it was blisteringly cold outside but Paul, Anna and the twins bundled up and pressed their way to Sunday service. They had been attending service faithfully and they never let a little bad weather stop them. The twins were one year old and they were accustomed to taking a nap every day around noon. The younger twin got very agitated that Sunday and began to cry uncontrollably because he couldn't take his nap because of all the music and singing that was going on that day. Anna suggested to Paul that she just leave with the children and return later to pick him up. Paul wasn't going to have it! He snatched the little boy up and hurriedly took him outside. The service ended and Paul and his son had not returned. Anna took the other baby and met them outside. Paul strapped both kids in their car seats and they returned home.

Anna began to undress the children after church so they could sit down and eat Sunday dinner when she noticed blood running profusely down his leg. She examined him closely and saw that both of his legs were bleeding because they had long lacerations on both of them.

Anna screamed, "Paul, why is Mickey's leg bleeding like this?" "What happened?" Paul told Anna he whipped him for acting up at church and they were welts and they would go away. Anna became very angry and rushed out of the house with the kids. Anna drove to her grandmother's house where they were having dinner with relatives that had come far and near. She sat down and started crying when a relative asked her what was wrong. Anna explained that Paul had whipped

Mickey and as a result his legs were bleeding. At that point everyone came in the living room where Anna was holding Mickey. They examined him and immediately became so angry that they wanted to retaliate against Paul. A few family members even took pictures with their cell phones. Anna tried to calm everyone down and assure them that she wouldn't let it happen again. Anna's cousin from Georgia who was a social worker suggested that she report Paul to Child Protective Services. Anna didn't want to do it because she was afraid that the children might end up in foster care. Mickey's twin sister Nickey was playing with her cousins and had no idea what all the uproar was about. Anna gathered Mickey and Nickey and they sat at the table to eat Sunday dinner.

When Anna and the children finally returned home, Paul was positioned on the living room sofa watching television as he normally did. She didn't have anything to say to Paul and went directly to the kids' room to put them in bed. Anna was so angry she slept with the kids that night.

"Anna! Why are you in here with the kids? Come to bed."

"Paul please leave me alone. I don't have anything to say. You just need to get some help for your temper."

"Get help? So you're mad because I disciplined my boy for acting a fool at church? Is that what this is all about? You done lost your mind. If I don't correct these kids, society will. But have your way and if he grow up and whip your ass, don't call me!"

Early Monday morning, Anna heard Paul leaving for work. She didn't bother to get up like she usually did. Nickey and Mickey woke up shortly after the door closed. It was time to get the day started. She gave them their morning bath, dressed them and fed them before dressing herself. After Anna and the kids were dressed she let them play while she cleaned.

About noon, there was a knock on the door. Anna peeped out the peep hole to see a strange woman standing there with a black notebook. Anna looked out the window to get a closer view when she noticed the lady was driving a white car with the county emblem on the door. She opened the door and the lady said, "I'm Crystal Brown from Child Protective Services. Are you Anna?"

"Yes I am," Anna answered.

"Is your husband here? We received an anonymous call that your son has possibly been abused."

"No, he's working." They sat down and the Social Worker asked if she could see Mickey. She examined him and took pictures of the lacerations on his legs.

Paul was angry with Anna because he thought she had reported him to CPS. Anna had not reported him and she didn't know who did but it could have been anyone at the Sunday dinner. There were a lot of people angry with Paul.

If Paul and Anna wanted to keep custody of their children they would have to follow CPS guidelines. Paul was ordered to take a psychiatric evaluation, months of anger management classes and parenting classes. When every detail was met and satisfied by CPS, Anna and Paul were happy that they wouldn't have to deal with the random visits anymore. Paul assured Anna that his anger was under control and she wouldn't have to worry about him abusing the kids.

Chapter 6

Anna decided to enroll in college once again. She had a major courseload of online courses and one face-to-face on Tuesday and Thursday nights. Anna was determined to get a higher education and hopefully a good paying job would follow. She spent a considerable amount of time online completing homework and browsing social media sites in her down time. Anna logged on to Facebook and received a message from a gentleman; Wesley, whom she had never talked to before.

"Hi beautiful. How are you today? he started.

"Hi. I'm great. How are you?

"My day just got a lot better since I'm talking to you sweetheart."

"Hmmm. Ok, that's sweet but I'm a married woman."

"And I'm a married man. I just wanted to tell you how beautiful your pictures are and that smile of yours, wow. It brightens up my day.

Anna didn't send another response. She just wasn't interested in talking to anyone. Besides, he had a wife and she had a husband. *What good could become of this*? she thought. A week later Wesley sent Anna another message. He apologized for coming on too strong but at the same time he suggested they talk on the phone. Wesley explained to Anna that he too was married and he and his wife were having marital problems so he just needed someone to talk to. Anna also felt that she might need someone to talk to as well. She and Paul were getting along but she didn't feel the same loving way about him as she did in the past.

> *I guess it wouldn't hurt to chat with him,* Anna began to convince herself.

Wesley told Anna that she would probably reach his assistant and it would be okay to give her name. When Anna called Wesley, he answered with a strong, deep, sexy voice.

Anna and Wesley began to call each other every day, even in the middle of the night when their spouses were asleep. Their conversations had escalated from friendly to sexual. Wesley wanted to meet Anna in person so he asked her to meet him for lunch in a nearby city and she agreed. Anna arrived at the restaurant first and waited anxiously for Wesley. When he arrived he got out and greeted Anna with a firm hug and a gentle kiss on the cheek. He told Anna he was pleasantly impressed. She was beautiful. He put his arm around her waist and they walked in the restaurant for lunch. They laughed and had a great conversation as they always did but this time they could look in each other's eyes and hold hands. Anna really liked Wesley and he obviously felt the same way about her. They didn't want to leave each other that day but he had to get home and Anna had to pick the kids up from her aunt's before Paul got home from work.

Just a few weeks later Wesley and Anna agreed to meet for lunch again. This time she went to the city he worked in because he didn't want to take another full day off. When Anna was almost there, Wesley called her and told her he had a surprise waiting..

"Hey baby, I know you're not expecting this but I really want to spend the rest of the day with you. I got us a room at the Marrion Hotel and I've already ordered room service. Don't be afraid. I just want us to be able to relax and get comfortable."

When Anna arrived at the hotel room, Wesley greeted her at the door and gave her an innocent kiss on the cheek.

"Come baby, this is for you." They sat down to a hot gourmet meal prepared by the hotel chef. Wesley popped open a bottle of Moscato and toasted "to good friends and stimulating conversation."

"Anna, I really think I'm in love with you."

Anna laughingly responded, "Wesley you're not in love with me. You just want to have sex."

"No, really Anna, I've never met a woman like you. You make me feel good. You always know exactly what to say to brighten up my day. I can't go a day without having you on my mind. I feel like you really understand me and I understand you and everything that you've been through. When I get up in the middle of the night, you're the first thing I think about. When I'm driving to work every morning, I'm thinking about you.

Anna looked him in the eye and said, "Wesley, honestly, I feel the same way about you."

When Wesley began to kiss Anna, she knew she didn't want to back out of what was about to happen. Wesley took her by the hand and pulled her towards him as he sat on the edge of the bed. Anna pushed him back on the bed as she stratled across his erect body, passionately kissing him wherever she could. Wesley unbuttoned her blouse and began to suck on her neck and her breasts. Anna pulled Wesley's shirt off and kissed him all over his chest. She felt that he was ready to go further. Wesley gently removed Anna's panties and began to kiss her from her ankles up to her inner thighs. He told her to relax as he pushed her legs further apart.

"Baby I've been waiting for this day. I've been waiting to take care of you," Wesley said as he began to make love to Anna. They made love like it was going to be the last time.

The unfaithful duo realized they had lost track of time when both of their phones continued to vibrate. They didn't want to, but they knew they had to go home.

Anna and Wesley fell in love and continued their affair well into a year until Wesley's wife ran across emails between the two of them. She began her own investigation, ultimately finding out everything she wanted to know about her husband and his mistress. Wesley loved Anna but he wasn't going to lose his wife. They both had great jobs, graduate degrees, a beautiful home, rental properties, independent businesses, luxury vehicles and years invested in their marriage. Wesley wasn't going to lose all that he had worked for, for Anna.

Before offering Anna a "severance package," Wesley explained to Anna that he truly loved her but he couldn't abandon his wife and children. He knew she was hurt because he knew she loved him too. Wesley told Anna to come to his job so he could officially say goodbye. Anna wasn't trying to meet Wesley to say goodbye. She was angry and if it was over, let it be over. Wesley pleaded with Anna and told her he wanted to present her with a special gift. Anna waited for Wesley in the parking deck. He walked up to her car and told her to get out. They began to embrace each other while tears flowed from their eyes.

"Anna, I'm so sorry it has to end this way. I'll always love you and no matter where I am in life I will always remember the wonderful times we had together. I just have to protect my investments and be there for my kids." Anna continued to sob as Wesley gave her a yellow envelope.

"Anna, I want you to have this. It's just a token of my love for you." He kissed Anna on her forehead and walked away. Anna got in her car and continued to cry all the way home. All she could think about was Wesley and all the wonderful times they had over the past year. Anna was hurt but she couldn't let it show when she got home to Paul. When she got home she remembered the yellow envelope in the seat. She thought Wesley had probably written her a note so she opened it to see what it said. It was a note and another piece of paper.

The note read, "Please take care of yourself. Buy you something nice. Love W.C."

Anna flipped the other piece of paper over to see that Wesley had given her a certified money order for $5000. Anna pulled back out the driveway to go call him. His assistant told her he had left for the day. She called his cell phone and he had changed his number. She knew for sure it was over. Wesley had told Anna that he had that number for eight years. Anna deposited the money order into her bank account and went back home.

She tried several times but was never able to reach Wesley again. It took her months to get over him and even after a year she still thought of him and what he was doing with his life but she never tried to reach him again.

Chapter 7

Anna was in class when she received a disturbing phone call from her friend Phylicia. "Anna I think you need to get home right away. Devin and I just left your house and Paul was extremely angry with Mickey. He knocked him down on the floor and choked him. Mickey was beginning to turn blue when Devin pulled him off of him! Your husband is crazy and you need to get home with your kids right away!"

Anna left everything on her desk and ran out of the building. When she got home she ran to Mickey's room where he laid still in his bed. Her heart was pounding from the fear that he might be dead. She was screaming to Paul, "What did you do to my son?"

"I didn't do anything, what the hell are you talking about?" Paul said.

"You choked him and I'm calling the police!" Mickey was breathing, but Anna was hysterical at the mere thought of Paul choking him. The police arrived and Anna explained to them that her friends were there with Paul and witnessed him choking Mickey until his face changed colors. The police examined Mickey as he lay asleep in his bed. One officer pulled Anna to the side and told her that there was no physical evidence that Mickey had been choked but if she felt that he was being abused in any way she should leave and seek further help.

The officers left and Anna and Paul fought for hours. Paul left early for work. Anna couldn't think of anything but what had happened, what could have happened and what actions she needed to take. She decided that it was time to leave Paul for good. How could she live with a man that she couldn't trust to be alone with his own children? What if no one is there the next time to pull him off of the kids when he gets angry?

Anna didn't have any savings and her income was very limited. She didn't know how she would survive on her own after being married to and dependent on Paul for 15 years. Paul was furious with Anna for calling the police. He packed some of his clothes and left without saying a word.

Anna decided that her only option was to sell everything she owned, even her furniture and some of her clothes. She was determined to find a safe place for herself and her children. It didn't matter that they would have to start over with nothing as long as they were at peace.

Two years later Paul had been frequently visiting Anna and the children. They would occasionally go on day trips to a mall, out to dinner or to the park. He tried fervently to persuade Anna he was a changed man. Paul desperately wanted his family back, but for Anna it was too late. She was content with the friendship they had but she didn't want anything more. She was about to finish school and she had found peace and serenity living on her own. Paul did all he could to prove to Anna that he could be trusted with the kids.

Paul began to stay with Anna on Tuesday and Thursday nights when her mother couldn't babysit so she could attend school. He lived out of town so it was more convenient for him to sleep on the sofa and leave for work from her house. Anna was in her last semester of college and she was preparing to start her internship when the unthinkable happened. Paul was watching the children while Anna was at school. Anna's mother came late that night because Anna needed her to babysit while she started her first day of her internship the next day. Anna returned home from class and talked to her mother and Paul about how excited she was to begin her internship as a Social Worker. She got her clothes out for her big day, took a shower, took a Tylenol PM, her antidepressants and got in bed. Paul fell asleep on the sofa and Anna's mother was in the bedroom adjacent to hers with the children. In the wee hours of the morning, Anna was lying asleep on her stomach when she was awakened by Paul on her back. He pushed Anna's head into the pillow, holding it down with his arm across the back of her neck while his hand covered her mouth.

"Be quiet, you don't want your mother to hear you screaming do you? You see the door is open."

He ripped Anna's panties off and began to sodomize her as she laid there, her pillow soaking in tears. The medicine Anna took had her too weak and drowsy to fight back. Anna wouldn't have screamed even if she could. She was too embarrassed for her mother to know what Paul was doing to her. When he finished torturing and raping Anna, he pulled his pants up and returned to the sofa as if nothing had happened. Anna made her way to the bathroom so she could clean up the blood that was all over her nightgown. Paul left for work before the sun came up. Anna got up and got dressed and left for her internship. As she drove down the highway tears flowed uncontrollably down her cheeks.

"How could he do that to me in my house, practically in front of my mother and kids?" "Does he hate me that much?" "Did I deserve that?" "What do I do now?"

Anna felt betrayed once again by Paul. He not only sexually assaulted her, but he emotionally and mentally destroyed her that night. She got to her destination but could not find the strength to go in. She started her car and returned home.

"Why are you back so soon?" her mother asked.

"Ma, I don't feel good and I've got to lie down for a while." Anna laid in bed all day crying, trying to figure out what went wrong. Her professor called to see why she didn't show up on-site but she wouldn't return any of her messages. Anna had had a mental breakdown.

Anna cut off all communication with Paul. He apologized for losing control but his apology did nothing for Anna's sanity. She felt nothing but hatred and disgust for him. She wouldn't allow him back in her home for any reason.

A couple of months later, Anna reapplied for the Social Work program but the board decided that it would be best if she switched majors. Anna confidentially confided in her professor and the head of the Social Work department about the situation that took place but they told her that she was too emotional and she didn't possess the characteristics of a good Social Worker. Her heart was broken and it seemed that everything she had been working towards was falling apart. She didn't want to switch majors but Sociology seemed to be the only other option when it came to obtaining a degree in a timely manner.

Anna couldn't afford an attorney but she was adamant in her decision to divorce Paul. She researched all the information she needed to draw up her own divorce documents. She filed for and was granted a divorce in less than 40 days. She felt relieved to finally be free, legally free from Paul.

Chapter 8

Anna wanted to start dating but she knew she had to get in shape. She wanted to look good and feel good about her body. She met with an old friend and personal trainer, Ryan Cross. He suggested that she meet him for lunch so they could go over a plan to help her get her figure back.

"Hi Anna, how are you? Are you excited about transforming into the woman you want to become?"

"Yes Ryan. Absolutely. I'm very excited. As you can see I've let myself go since I saw you last."

"Don't worry about that Anna. You're still beautiful and when I'm done with you, you won't be able to keep the men off. Honestly, I'd take you just as you are."

Anna dropped her head with the biggest smile on her face. It had been a long time since a man made her feel attractive.

"I'm serious. I think you're beautiful and your weight doesn't bother me. I love thick women."

"Of course you do Ryan, "she said sarcastically.

"You know what Anna, I'm going to take you out this weekend and I'm not taking no for an answer. You've got me all wrong sweetheart. Yes, my career is in fitness but you have to understand that what I'm looking for in a woman is much more than her outer appearance. I've known you for a very long time Anna and you've always carried yourself as a real woman. You're educated, goal oriented, sensitive, honest, a wonderful mother...should I go on? I need someone like you. I'll pick you up Saturday at seven."

"Ok Ryan that will be great and thanks for lunch. I'll see you Saturday."

Ryan arrived promptly at 7:00 p.m. Anna opened the door and he was looking delicious. He was dressed in black jeans, a white nicely pressed shirt and a leather jacket. His masculine physique pierced through his clothing and his bald head was glistening under the night lights. Anna had on a tight fitting, red, knee length dress that hugged her curvaceous body gracefully. From the look in his eyes, Ryan was very pleased. He escorted Anna to the passenger side and opened the door just like she liked it. Anna didn't know exactly what he had planned so she just sat back in his Cadillac Escalade and enjoyed the ride.

"I've discovered this great steakhouse in Greenville where the food is always delicious. It'll take us about 45 minutes to get there so relax and tell me how your day was."

"Ryan I had a wonderful day. As you know, I've been working from home so I did some billing and coding while the kids are at my mother's. I did a little shopping earlier, got a medi/pedi and as you can see I got my hair done. Do you like it?"

"I like it and everything about you," he said.

Anna turned her head and looked out the window with a huge smile on her face. "Thank you, you're so kind Ryan."

After dinner Ryan and Anna decided to see a movie. They barely made it to the 10 o'clock show. Anna didn't want to tell Ryan on their first real date that she didn't like going to movies after 7 p.m. She would always fall asleep; nevertheless, she was determined to make it through the movie this time. Ryan held Anna's hand throughout the entire movie. He leaned over and gave her a gentle kiss on the cheek as the credits began roll.

"Did you enjoy the movie baby?"

"Yes, I did. Surprisingly I didn't go to sleep. That's the first time in years," she said jokingly.

It was well past midnight and the drive home was extremely quiet. Anna wasn't used to being out that late and she became very sleepy. Ryan didn't seem to mind if she got some rest on the way home. He played some soft jazz music, just loud enough to enjoy but soft enough not to disturb her. Ryan was very masculine yet every action towards Anna was remarkably gentle and kind.

Ryan didn't wake Anna until he was parked in her driveway. "Wake up sweetheart, you're home. Let me walk you in." Anna got out of the truck and Ryan closed the door behind her. They slowly walked hand in hand to the door. She thanked him for a lovely night and laughingly apologized for falling asleep.

"That's no big deal honey. I enjoyed you as well and I look forward to taking you out again real soon." He gave her a gentle kiss on the cheek and wished her a good night. "I'll call you tomorrow Anna."

Anna never complied with the weight loss goals she and Ryan had agreed upon. She became comfortable with him and he seemed happy with her just as she was. They continued to date and ultimately agreed on a monogamous relationship. He always treated Anna with kindness and respect and she reciprocated the same towards him. Anna wanted this relationship to last and she wasn't trying to do anything to end it. She felt that Ryan could really be the man of her dreams.

The alarm went off at 5 a.m. as it usually did when Ryan would spend the night with Anna. He took a shower and got dressed.

"Have a wonderful Tuesday sweetheart. Don't work too hard baby," Anna said as Ryan was leaving for work.

"Thanks sweet cheeks. I can't wait to see you Friday."

Ryan and Anna would normally talk throughout the week, anticipating an enjoyable night of dinner, dancing and cocktails every Friday. This particular week was different. Anna called Ryan several times and he hurried off the phone. He explained that he had several new clients and they were keeping him extremely busy. He would usually call her after work to see if she needed anything like bread, milk or eggs. He didn't ask at all that week. Anna had doubts about his new behavior, but she tried to convince herself that it was just her imagination.

Friday morning, Ryan confirmed that he would pick Anna up at seven. At 7:30, he called and told Anna he would be running a little late because he was experiencing some symptoms of a stomach virus. He knew she would be sympathetic and voluntarily cancel their plans. He knew Anna had a big and caring heart.

A couple of hours after canceling their date, Anna went to the supermarket to buy Ryan some ginger ale and crackers. Her intention was to swing by his apartment and drop it off like any loving girlfriend would do. She wasn't going to risk catching a virus but she genuinely cared about his well-being. Anna pulled up in his driveway and what do you know, his truck was gone. She called him repeatedly but with no resolution.

"He's up to something no good," she thought. On her way home, it hit her! *"I bet his lying ass is at the movie theater."* Unsurprisingly, Anna pulled up to the theater parking lot and there it was. His shiny, black Cadillac Escalade. Her heart was pounding but she tried to think positive. *"What if he didn't want me to know he was going out with his buddies? What if he just wanted to see a movie alone tonight? Did he loan his truck to a friend? There's got to be a good explanation and I'm going to wait and see what it is,* she reasoned to herself.

Anna reluctantly parked beside his truck and waited for him or whoever it could have been to walk out. The movie ended and the parking lot was almost empty. There was still no sign of Ryan. A few minutes later she saw Ryan walking towards his truck, but he was not alone.

"So this is why you've been so distant? You're seeing my friend of all people."

"Anna, it's not what it looks like! We're just friends."

"Just friends, huh? You told me you were sick, but I find you at the movie with Christy? How could you do me like this? And Christy, you are just trifling. Anna and Christy had been friends for a few years. Anna had attended a few parties that Christy hosted and they had something in common like so many of Anna's friends. They both had bad luck with men. Anna had just told Christy the week before that she was in a relationship with Ryan, but little did she know that Christy was dating him behind her back. Christy didn't care about Anna's feelings. She was a selfish, coldhearted tramp that would date any man for a dollar and sex. Ryan opened the passenger door for Christy so she could sit safely inside his truck while he proceeded to break off his relationship with Anna.

"Like I said Anna, we are just friends but at the same time I'm not going to tolerate you confronting me or following me or whatever you call this! You are crazy! This was not necessary and it's best that we end it right here!"

"Oh, really? Okay Ryan. No problem. Do what makes you happy."

Anna sped away, angry, hurt and disappointed. Those feelings were becoming all too familiar and Anna vowed that night to never allow it to happen again.

Chapter 9

The big day arrived and Anna was ecstatic about her college graduation. Her dreams of becoming a Social Worker were put aside but a degree in Sociology was better than nothing at all. She could always pursue a graduate degree in Social Work later on. As she walked across the stage she felt a sense of accomplishment that she hadn't felt in a very long time. She looked up in the stadium seats with a smile on her face. Her mother and three children were there cheering for her and it felt wonderful to set an example of endurance and perseverance.

She didn't celebrate with an after party, a big graduation dinner or any other extravagant event. Instead, she ordered take-out for herself and the twins. Anna's mother and daughter went their separate ways and it was business as usual. She was happy that she had earned her bachelor's degree, but before nightfall she started to feel extremely lonely. She missed the companionship of a man, the late night conversations, the good morning and goodnight texts, the random calls just to say hello and most of all she missed dating.

"Why is it so hard to find Mr. Right? Does he exist for me or should I give up on finding love? I know I'm a good woman...I know this! I guess I'm too fat for most men. Yeah, that's it, she thought.

Every man Anna had dated treated her bad in one way or another. She had been abused, used, and emotionally torn apart by men. Anna didn't want to be hurt again, but she longed so desperately to be loved and accepted for the kind, gentle and caring woman she was.

"I don't want to be hurt again...I'm scared to give myself to anyone else. Have I been cursed for all the wrong I've done in my life?"

Anna dropped the kids off at school and returned home to get dressed for a job interview. As she was backing out of the driveway the temp agency called.

"Ms. Paxton, unfortunately, we filled the position late yesterday afternoon. We were impressed with your resume, however; the other candidate was more qualified for the position," the caller said.

"Yeah, I've heard that a million times," Anna thought. She pulled back in the driveway and it began to pour down rain. *Now what am I going to do today? I guess I'll get on FibBook and see what everyone's lying about today.* Anna got on the social media site and within minutes she got an instant message from a guy named Rico. Anna didn't know him and didn't even remember becoming his friend on FibBook. Nevertheless, she was bored and he was kind of cute so why not be entertained. Rico was a wonderful conversationalist. He wasn't boring like all the other guys she had chatted with. Anna hadn't laughed that hard in a long time and she hadn't even heard his voice. Rico wanted to continue their conversation over the phone and Anna was more than willing to oblige. Rico called

Anna and they talked for hours about any and everything. Rico asked Anna what type of man she was interested in.

"Rico I can tell you what I don't want better than I can tell you what I do want. First of all, he can't have a criminal record. He cannot be a drinker or do drugs. He has to be single. He must be God-fearing. He needs to be honest and faithful and he has to be a hard worker."

Rico listened attentively as Anna spoke diligently of the characteristics she didn't want in a man.

"Would you date a man who did those things but wanted to stop?"

"Rico, I could be friends with someone like that but nothing more. I couldn't be serious with someone that possibly couldn't find a job because of his criminal past. I've never dated anyone that smoked and drank and I'm not going to start now. If they want to stop I prefer they do it before I get involved with them."

"I see. Well, I have been to prison Anna…actually a couple of times. I have a job and I'm trying to get my life together. I need a woman like you. You're different from the women I've been involved with. I need someone like you in my life."

"When and why were you in prison Rico? Did you kill someone?"

"No baby. I used to sell drugs but that life is behind me now. I'm trying to be a better man."

Anna put Rico on hold to check the state's department of corrections website for his criminal background history. She wasn't going to entertain a murderer or a robber. Rico's record showed exactly what he said. *"What a relief. Somewhat anyway."*

"Rico how old are you?"

"I'm 33, but I'm an old soul. Is that a problem?" he asked.

"Well, considering we're just looking for friendship I don't see where it makes a difference."

Rico asked Anna to go out with him on a date that weekend. She was a bit apprehensive in accepting his invitation but she decided to say yes. It was just a date with a new friend, she thought. She wasn't looking for love, not with him anyway, just a good time.

Rico and Anna continuously talked throughout the week, sharing their favorite music and ideas with one another. They were both anxious to meet in person fearing that one may not like the other. As usual, Anna feared that Rico would think she was fat and unattractive. He had already assured Anna that her size didn't matter, but she didn't believe him.

Anna prepared for her date. She didn't get dressed up like she normally would. She liked Rico's conversation but she knew the most she could have with him was a casual friendship. She definitely didn't feel the need to dress to impress. Rico arrived promptly at Anna's house. He called her to tell her he was outside. Anna looked at Danielle who was there to babysit her brother and sister and asked, "Do you mean to tell me he's not coming to the door to get me? He wants me to just get in his car? What kind of foolishness is this? I'll go this time but it will be the last! I'm not used to this!" Anna grabbed her purse and proceeded to walk to Rico's car. He simultaneously got out and greeted her; however, he didn't open the door for her. She tried to think positive and enjoy her date with Rico regardless of his lack of gentleman like behavior.

Rico took Anna to dinner at a local steakhouse where they engaged in a fun and enjoyable conversation. Rico was such a hilarious character. Anna was really enjoying his company and it was evident that he was enjoying hers as well. They concluded the date with a movie and a walk in the park. Anna felt like she had known Rico forever. He was different from any man she had dated. He was fun, humorous and intelligent and most of all he brought a little happiness to her life. She wasn't looking for a love connection in Rico but she definitely wanted to see him again.

Rico walked Anna in and he gave her a strong hug and sweet kiss on her lips. Danielle had taken her brother and sister home with her so Anna asked Rico to stay a while longer. Their chemistry was magnificent and neither of them wanted the night to end. They talked, laughed and ultimately fell asleep on the sofa.

As the weeks progressed, Rico and Anna became exceptionally close. Anna was a little apprehensive when Rico asked her to commit to a monogamous relationship but she put her guard down and accepted his offer. They discovered more and more secrets of each other's past. He revealed to Anna that he had four children by three women and that he was still legally married; however separated from his wife. They had become emotionally, physically and sexually bonded but Anna decided it was time to call off their now committed relationship. She was beginning to sense that Rico was not being honest with her about many other things and she felt he was not being faithful. She confronted him about her worries and he assured her that she was just paranoid and he was not seeing anyone else. Shortly thereafter, Rico disappeared for five days straight. He had his cellphone turned off and Anna could not reach him. She knew he was with another woman and accepted the fact that their relationship was over. On the sixth day, Rico appeared at Anna's door, full of apologies and excuses. She didn't want to hear anything he had to say. He pleaded with her to give him another chance. Anna had strong feelings for Rico and felt she owed the relationship another chance. On the ninth day Anna continuously called Rico, but he would not answer. That was it for Anna. She was not going to put up with his disrespect any longer. Rico disappeared again for four days this time before contacting Anna. She explained to Rico that whatever he had been doing, he should go back and keep doing it because she was done. He constantly called Anna, leaving apologetic messages on her voicemail. He told her he loved her and he was not letting her go. He said things were not as they seemed and he swore on his kid's life that he had not been with another woman. Once again, Anna took him back. She promised him that if he did not change, she would permanently leave him alone. Rico began to stay with Anna almost six days a week providing her with some sort of comfort in believing he was trying to make their relationship work.

Rico invited Anna to his family's cookout one Saturday. He wanted her to meet his entire family at once. He got out of bed and told Anna he would come back to pick her up in a few hours. Twenty minutes after Rico left Anna, he texted her. "It's not four, it's seven," the text read.

Anna was busy getting dressed and didn't have time to text, so she called him. "Seven what? What are you talking about?"

"You're going to be mad Anna, but I have seven children by five different women. I know someone is going to mention it to you today so I'm coming clean." "Rico, you should not be ashamed to tell me or anyone else that you have seven kids. They came along before me, they're yours and you shouldn't try to hide that. Any woman that truly loves you will accept your children too." Anna could hear how relieved Rico was by the tone of his voice. Anna continued to get her twins dressed and they waited on Rico to return. He called a few hours later and told Anna if she still wanted to go to the cookout, she was welcome to drive on her own. He said he had to pick up three of his kids and it wasn't enough room for Anna and her kids. Anna refused to show up as to appear as if she had invited herself to his family's cookout. She wasn't going for it! *This is exactly why I should have left this boy alone!* she thought.

Anna continued her relationship with Rico for several months regardless of the emotional and mental damage he was causing her. She had fallen in love with him and didn't want to let him go. She kept holding on to his promises to change for the better but his actions proved otherwise. Nothing had hurt Anna more than receiving a message on

FibBook from a woman who told her she was involved with Rico. She told Anna that Rico was tired of her and her nagging. She told Anna that Rico was making love to her on a regular basis because her sex was better and Rico wasn't going to stop being with her. She insulted Anna in every way possible. She called her fat, ugly and irritating. After confronting Rico about the message, he denied knowing the lady and having any involvement with her.

Anna ultimately caught Rico spending the night with one of his kids' mothers. He said he fell asleep while visiting his son and he had not had sex with the woman. Anna didn't believe him and broke up with him right away. As usual, Rico begged her not to leave him. He said it wasn't what it looked like. This was the first of many times he was found spending the night with his child's mother and every time he used the same excuse. Anna found out that they had never stopped sleeping together and he was taking her out of town with him on the weekends. Anna had finally had enough! She felt betrayed by the man she loved with her whole heart. She became angry for allowing herself to get emotionally bound with someone who she knew was not what she wanted from the beginning.

Rico suddenly moved in with the woman he was seeing, spending quality time with her, his son and her other children. Anna had no choice but to move on with her life.

Chapter 10

The winter came and Anna had got her first bad cold of the season. Her body ached and nothing she took seemed to relieve her pain. She lay in bed for a few days extremely sick and ultimately experiencing nausea and vomiting. She hadn't felt that way in seven years. She was pregnant with Mickey and Nickey the last time she experienced those symptoms. Anna looked at her calendar and realized she hadn't had a menstrual period in over a month but she wasn't concerned about being pregnant because she had a tubal ligation when she gave birth to the twins. Anna fell asleep on her sofa and dreamed that she had a baby. She woke up startled and confused. *"What if they didn't do the procedure right? What if I am pregnant?"* Anna wanted to make sure she wasn't, so she went to buy a pregnancy test. The test showed up positive, but Anna just couldn't accept it. She called Rico and informed him that she had taken a pregnancy test and it was positive. He became very angry. He told her if she was pregnant by him she better not have it because he didn't want any more kids.

"I thought your tubes were tied. How can you be pregnant?" he asked.

"I don't know Rico, but I'll just go buy another test to make sure." Anna got off the phone and went to the drugstore. *Wow, this seems so familiar*, she thought, remembering the same scenario seven years earlier.

"Rico, I took the second test and it's positive as well."

"You're going to have to get rid of it. I don't want any more kids and if you plan on keeping it I'll never have anything to do with you or the child.

"I don't care what you say Rico. I'm not getting an abortion. You don't want to be in our life, fine. You can go on with your life. I don't need you and I can raise the baby by myself. You don't ever have to worry about being in the baby's life."

Rico didn't want to hear anything Anna had to say. He told her to get rid of it or else. Rico didn't want an eighth child and furthermore he didn't want it to interfere with his current relationship. He told Anna that if she kept the baby she better not call him until it was born. Anna's eyes filled with tears. She didn't know what to do but she knew she didn't believe in abortions and she wasn't going to get one.

Rico called Anna every day from work begging her to get an abortion. He cried and pleaded with her not to have his baby. He told her he was leaving his girlfriend and he wanted her back but he wasn't coming back if she kept the baby.

"Rico I might not be pregnant. The pregnancy tests could have been wrong. I know for a fact I got my tubes tied. I'm making a doctor's appointment tomorrow to see what's going on."

"Anna, if you're not pregnant we can get back together. I just don't want another baby! I can't stress that enough. I don't want another one!"

Anna called her gynecologist to schedule an appointment. She couldn't understand how she had two positive pregnancy tests when her tubes were tied. The nurse told Anna an appointment wasn't necessary and that she could walk right in. When she arrived at the doctor's off, she took her third pregnancy test and it was positive.

"How can I be pregnant when I got a tubal ligation seven years ago?"

"Ms. Paxton, Dr. Vaughn is going to want you to have a pelvic ultrasound. Let me get everything sat up for you."

Anna waited in the examination room for Dr. Vaughn.

"Ms. Paxton, I'm looking over your medical records and apparently you never consented to a tubal ligation."

"Dr. Vaughn I can assure you I was supposed to have my tubes tied when I had my C-section seven years ago," Anna explained.

"I'm sorry Ms. Paxton but there is nothing in your records. I'm going to send you down the hall to get a pelvic ultrasound. Maybe that can help shed some light on what's going on here."

"Ms. Paxton, I need to apply a cool gel to your abdomen before I can proceed with the ultrasound." As the ultrasound technician scanned Anna's abdomen, she became very anxious.

"Ma'am, do you see anything? Am I pregnant? Please tell me. I need to know now!" Anna exclaimed.

"Yes you are Ms. Paxton. Look at the monitor. This is your baby and according to the measurements you are approximately 5 to 6 weeks pregnant."

All Anna could hear in her mind was Rico pleading with her to get an abortion. She knew if she told him that the doctor confirmed the pregnancy that he would be furious. Anna was torn between choosing a future relationship with Rico and aborting a baby neither of them wanted. All of her life, Anna was totally against abortion and counseled other people to spare the lives of their innocent babies.

As Anna was leaving the doctor's office Rico called to see what the outcome was. Anna had to think quickly. She didn't want to upset him and risk losing him forever.

"Rico, I have good news. It was a false alarm. I'm not pregnant. I guess it was something in my system, maybe some medication, which was causing a false-positive result."

"Wow, you had me worried. I just can't see myself with 8 kids!" Rico said with a sigh of relief.

Anna kept her pregnancy a secret from Rico, her family and even her best friend for several weeks. Rico continued his relationship with his girlfriend although he promised Anna he would be with her. They appeared to be very much in love. Anna's friends would tell her how Rico and his newfound family would spend days cooking out and spending quality time together. Anna wanted a relationship with Rico, but clearly he had lied about wanting to be with her. He was happy and she wasn't going to interfere. Her heart was crushed and the disappointment of carrying his baby without his knowledge was overwhelming.

Anna was approaching 16 weeks into her pregnancy. She knew she had to make a decision. *Should I get an abortion or not?* she questioned.

Anna cried every day at the very thought of killing her unborn child, but she couldn't financially or emotionally support another child alone. Rico obviously wasn't going to support them either. He had already told her if she had his baby he would hate her for the rest of her life.

Anna decided to browse the internet for abortion information. She found out that she could have an abortion up to 20 weeks. She decided it would be the best decision to get it done right away so she could carry on with her life. She made an appointment for the following week. Anna arranged for her mother to keep the twins for three days. She lied to her mother and told her that she would be visiting a friend.

Friday morning Anna checked into a hotel near the abortion clinic. She called a taxi to drop her off at her appointment and the taxi driver looked at her as she was paying him the fare.

"Ma'am, here's my personal cellphone number. Business is really slow today. Call me if you need a ride back to the hotel."

Anna began to cry as she thanked him for being so kind to her. She entered the clinic to proceed with what would be the most devastating thing she would ever experience.

Four hours later, she was no longer pregnant and it seemed liked all her problems would be solved. She would never have to tell anyone about the abortion. Rico wouldn't have to hate her for having his baby and maybe at some point in the future she would find the perfect man. After all, she had too many strikes against her. She was overweight. She already had young kids. And she felt she was getting old.

Ironically, Rico called Anna the very next morning. He said he wanted her to go with him out of town on a business trip.

"Rico, I'm sorry I can't go. I'm very sick."

"What's wrong with you?" he asked.

"I don't know. Maybe I have the flu. By the way, why are you calling me to go out of town with you? I haven't talked to you in weeks. What's going on?"

"Well, for one thing, I really miss you and another thing; I really need your help."

"So where's your girlfriend and why can't she help?"

"See Anna, you never let me explain that situation to you. You always assumed something was going on and in reality I wasn't even sleeping with her. She has some mental issues and I was there a lot for my son. She helped me out when my car broke down and it probably looked like I was living with her but I was just there to use her car for work. I know you don't believe me but honestly I wasn't having sex with her then and I'm not having sex with her now."

"You're right Rico! I don't believe that bullshit. Anyway I have to go. I'll talk to you later."

As the weeks went by, Anna experienced deep feelings of regret, loss, shamefulness, hopelessness and loneliness. She could no longer sleep at night. She was easily agitated and often times unusually forgetful. Daily she would think about what her son would have looked like. Would he have been like her or more like his daddy? Would he have big eyes like the rest of her kids? Every negative emotion possible began to manifest and Anna could no longer cope. She couldn't tell anyone because she was too ashamed. She didn't feel like God would ever forgive her for aborting her baby. Depression took over Anna's life.

Not a day went by that Anna didn't relive every negative event that ever happened in her life. She thought about Derrick and how he had abandoned her during her pregnancy with Danielle. She thought about how Paul cheated on her, tried to kill her, abused their children and said she wasn't a real woman. She thought about her failed relationships with Brian, Wesley, Ryan and now Rico. She felt that all these men had trampled her heart in one way or another. She constantly reached out to Paul for help with the kids but to no avail. When she used her last $1000 to get the abortion, it really put Anna in a financial strain. She had collection notices and calls coming in every day. She was down to nothing. She was financially, mentally, emotionally and physically drained.

Chapter 11

"This is it! I can't live like this! I'm a murderer. My baby, my baby! How could I have been so selfish?"

Anna could no longer cope with the fact that she had chosen to terminate her pregnancy. She felt she had lost it all! She continued to think back at all the hurt she had felt in past relationships. She had looked for love in all the wrong men. She had been abused, used and neglected. She no longer had a spiritual relationship with God like she had had the better part of her life. Everything that could possibly go wrong, had done just that. On top of every negative, unforgiving and worthless emotion Anna felt, nothing compared to the constant agony of knowing that she aborted an innocent child for her own personal satisfaction, including the possibility of a future relationship with Rico.

Anna emotionally and mentally hit rock bottom. *"The best way to end this pain and turmoil is to end my life,"* she thought. *"I'm not worthy of living. I'm not worthy of being a mother, a friend or anything else to anyone! I'm old, fat, ugly and no man will ever want me anyway. My kids will be better off with someone else. I'm a horrible person and I don't deserve to be here. Everyone will be much happier after I'm gone.*

Anna sat up all night contemplating the best way to commit suicide. She had tried pills before and that didn't work, so to insure a successful suicide she decided to jump off a bridge. She never learned how to swim so drowning was inevitable. Anna didn't have life insurance and she didn't want to leave a burial expense for her family to struggle with. She figured getting eaten by sharks would be the best solution to that problem. *No body, no bills.*

Anna took her children to school the next morning. She walked them to the door and gave them the biggest hug she had ever given. She looked them both in their faces and told them that no matter what, she loved them with her whole heart. She walked away with tears streaming down her face. She knew that would be her last time seeing her children. She texted Paul and told him he needed to pick the children up after school because she had a doctor's appointment. Her mother was going to keep the kids but she wouldn't be there until later that night. She knew that her mother would raise them well and love them as much as she loved them. Anna left all of their vital records on her bed so that her mother would have everything she needed to apply for benefits for the kids after she passed away.

Anna filled her car up with gas for what was now her final destination. She knew the perfect place to end her horrible life. Anna drove two hours to the James River in Newport News, Virginia. She cried the entire way thinking she was making the best decision for everyone and that she wasn't worthy to live. Anna approached the highest point of the bridge and began to slow down. She was going to stop her car there and jump. As Anna drastically reduced speed to almost five miles per hour, the persistent sounds of horns blowing, forced her to continue driving. Still considerate of others, Anna didn't want to be the reason so many people would be late for work or school. She continued to drive until she reached the end of the bridge. She noticed a park was located just to the left of the bridge with a connecting pier that extended over the river. She parked and walked to the edge of the river, faced drenched in tears. She stood there contemplating...

Anna couldn't find the nerve to fully submerge herself in the deep waters. For several hours onward, Anna walked back and forth from her car to the edge of the river. *It would have been so much easier to jump off the bridge,* she thought. Anna couldn't end her life like this. She realized suicide was not the solution to her problems. She got in her car for the last time and turned her cellphone on. She had forty-nine messages and texts. When she heard her mother's voice pleading for her to call, Anna immediately realized the hurt she would bring upon the hearts of all of those that loved her, especially her mother. Anna decided to give herself one more chance at life.

Anna returned home to be greeted by an angry Paul. He started calling her derogatory names and threatening to seek legal custody of their children. Anna began to doubt her decision to come home. This was just the beginning of more stress in Anna's life.

In the weeks to come, Anna tried to find peace and solidarity within. She was on a positive path of self-worth even after receiving a disturbing phone call from her friend Renee.

"Hey Anna, I just saw Rico and his girlfriend. She's pregnant. It looks like she's about five months."

Anna could not believe Rico got his sons' mother pregnant, after all he swore he was not sleeping with her. *"How could he do this when he didn't want me to have our baby? I had an abortion so that he wouldn't have the responsibility of another child, but now he's having one with her? Oh God! I feel so stupid, but I'm not going to let this get the best of me. I just can't.*

As Anna stood at her bathroom mirror reminiscing on her past, she realized how strong of a woman she really was.

I've been through so much in my life. I was a victim of domestic abuse; I didn't even know it. I was raped and didn't think I had any rights to report it. I know some women have experienced greater hurt and disappointment. Some of them didn't even live to tell their story, but I survived. I survived everything. My life will go on. I may be bent, but I'm not broken. I'm a survivor and I'm resilient. All my life I thought I couldn't be happy alone but I finally realize that I can create my own happiness. It starts within and it starts today. I will have a happily ever after.